UNBEARABLE

BAEN BOOKS
by A. LEE MARTINEZ

Unbearable

To purchase this title in e-book form, please go to baen.com.

UNBEARABLE

A. LEE MARTINEZ

BAEN

UNBEARABLE

This is a work of fiction. All the characters and events portrayed in this book are fictional, and any resemblance to real people or incidents is purely coincidental.

A Baen Books Original

Baen Publishing Enterprises
P.O. Box 1403
Riverdale, NY 10471
www.baen.com

ISBN: 978-1-6680-7345-2

Cover art by Todd Lockwood

First printing, September 2026

Distributed by Simon & Schuster
1230 Avenue of the Americas
New York, NY 10020

Library of Congress Control Number: 2026020601

Printed in the United States of America

10 9 8 7 6 5 4 3 2 1

Dedication:

To Mom, doing this without your steady support
would be a hell of a lot harder.

To Sally, I love you more every year.

To DFWWW, by far the greatest group of writers
I've ever had the honor of being associated with.
Also, the only group, but it still counts.

And to the Mighty Orbots.
Hey, it's hard coming up with cool
pop culture references that haven't been
done to death. You try it sometime.

UNBEARABLE

CHAPTER ONE

The spade broke the soft earth easily. I'd dug out a shallow trench and wasn't even tired. And I'd worried I'd eat a bullet sweaty and out of breath.

Roger sat on a rock, watching me with a pistol across his lap. I liked Roger. He was a good guy. Despite the situation, I still thought of us as friends.

"How deep do we want this?" I asked, tossing more dirt to the side.

"Deep enough that we don't have any arms or legs sticking out," he said.

"What about dogs?" I said. "Probably have to be fairly deep to avoid having dogs find me."

"What would dogs be doing out here?" he said.

"You never know. The road's just over that ridge. Someone ditches a dog at the edge of the woods. The poor thing is hungry and confused. Finds a tasty corpse to dig up."

Roger frowned. "Who would abandon a dog out here?"

"People do bad things."

"Yeah." He took a puff from his vape and scowled at the universe. "Fucking people. Just keep digging. I'll tell you when to stop."

As long as I was digging, there was always a chance things might change. I'd always been an optimist. Optimism had never been kind enough to return the favor. But I wasn't dead yet, and I had been meaning to get more exercise, and it was a nice night. Things could have been worse.

Irish luck, as my dad was fond of saying, though he wasn't Irish and never had an ounce of good fortune in his life.

"I don't really want to do this," said Roger.

"I know you don't," I said. "It's my fault, really. If that makes you feel any better about it."

"Kind of you to say."

"Just the truth," I replied. "We all dig our own graves." I tossed a shovelful of dirt. "Usually more metaphorical than this, though."

"Huh." He studied me like a curiosity; a three-legged dog, a parrot that knew how to swear. "That's kind of insightful."

"I have my moments," I said.

"Just surprising. See, I knew you weren't smart, Ortiz, but I didn't think you were stupid. But then you did the thing—"

"The thing was stupid," I agreed. "I can tell you where I stashed the money, if you want."

"I'd still have to kill you," he said. "Horace was very specific about that."

"Sure, but it'll make Horace happier if you bring it to him."

He shrugged. "Fuck Horace. He wants the money back so bad, he should have sent someone else."

"Aren't you worried he'll think you found and kept it?"

"He knows I'm not that stupid."

"No, that's a special kind of stupid," I agreed.

"Was she worth it?" asked Roger.

I rolled the question around in my head.

"No."

He cracked a grin under the pale light of the full moon, and I returned to digging.

My shovel sank deep into the ground, swallowing the spade whole. I tugged, but the earth refused to let it go. The shovel lowered itself inch by inch despite my best efforts. The tool was swallowed with a slurp and cloud of dust, like the hole was belching.

"What the hell?" asked Roger.

"I didn't do it," I said.

The ground bubbled as a black hole appeared where the shovel had disappeared. The earth fell away as the hole grew bigger. I scrambled out of my grave. Roger was nice enough to give me a hand. We peered into the bottomless opening. Its blackness consumed the moonlight.

"Some kind of sinkhole," said Roger. "You'd fallen into that, you'd have been killed."

"My lucky day," I said.

Roger was distracted. It would be easy enough to push him into the chasm. Something even I'd have trouble screwing up. But I liked Roger.

A blast of hot wind erupted from the hole as something shiny was ejected over our heads. It landed behind us.

"Is that a sword?" asked Roger.

It was. The weapon had driven itself into the ground, blade first, and now stood before us. I didn't know a lot about swords, but it didn't seem fancy. But the way the moonlight reflected off it was hypnotic, almost blinding.

Roger and I moved for it, but it was a few inches closer to me, so I reached it first. I pulled the blade from the ground, and the earth responded with a quake. The tremor knocked Roger off his feet, but not me. An urge to hold the sword above my head struck me, but I didn't want to look like an asshole, so I pushed it away.

Roger stood. "Let me see that."

"No."

The sword felt right in my hands. Like it was meant for me right now at this moment. Like it had been waiting all this time, under the earth, for me to come along.

He pointed the gun at me.

"I'm not through digging," I said.

"Eh, that's a pretty deep hole. Good-bye, Ortiz."

"Bye, Roger."

Before he could pull the trigger, the ground rumbled. A tall, thick tree uprooted itself, toppling over. It crushed Roger beneath it. His legs stuck out from under it like the Wicked Witch of the East. I couldn't see the rest of him.

"Hey, Roger," I said. "You okay down there?"

He didn't respond. His legs didn't even twitch.

Another blast of burning wind seared the forest. It was hot enough that the leaves on nearby trees blackened. A glowing hand reached over the edge of the sinkhole. It was followed by a glowing man in a suit. The figure stood, unbuttoned his coat.

He was made of light. Where there should've been flesh, there was a shimmering heat mirage. His eyes were two red points, and his mouth was a white swoosh. Each strand of his hair was a tiny rainbow.

"Hello." He wiped some of the dust from his clothes.

"Hi."

The man of light studied Roger's legs. "Friend of yours?"

"He was. Is he dead?" I don't know why I asked. Just trying to make conversation.

The man of light spoke quietly, but with purpose. He spoke, and the world quieted to listen to every word.

"Does it matter? If he lives, he learns. If he dies, he's just another speck of dust to be swept away in the sandstorm of time. You, on the other hand, have become very important. You found the sword. Or maybe it found you, Ortiz?"

"How do you know my name?"

He nodded to the fallen tree. "Overheard him."

"How long have you been down there?"

"A complicated question. How do I know I'm still not down there? How do I know that you are real, that any of this is real? I could ask you, but you'd probably lie to me."

He adjusted his sleeves, and paused to quietly inspect his own hands like foreign objects.

"You're not in the hole," I said.

"I guess I'll have to take your word for it."

A hot wind blew through the woods, but this time it went downward into the hole. The tree rolled off of Roger, splintered into pieces before being sucked into the void. Roger's corpse tumbled in right behind. It disappeared into the emptiness. The earth rose up, filling the hole once again.

"You probably have a lot of questions," said the man of light. "The short of it is that up to now, you've lived your life in the Waking World. But now you've entered the Dreaming World. Everything you thought you understood about your life, it's not true. It will take time to grasp, and you might not have that time. Sorry about that, but I've got a job to do. More of a calling, really."

He ran his hand through his rainbow hair, scattering prisms of color through the air. He literally flashed a smile at me. He was beautiful. It wasn't only his golden glow. It was the way he carried himself. He was a god pretending to be human, and maybe doing only an okay job of it, but still radiating power and grace and eternity. Above all, he felt eternal. Even the stars would burn out one day, but not him.

He was so bright, but something about him made it bearable. I wondered if it was like looking at an eclipse, and in three minutes I'd be blind, but I couldn't look away.

He said, "You have the sword."

The question broke the trance, and I stepped back.

"You can't have it."

"It was mine first," he said, "but circumstances seems to have blurred the rules of possession. I can feel it still, calling to me. Like it called to you."

"I was just digging a hole," I said. "I didn't even pick the spot. Roger did."

"But you have our sword."

My body tensed at the word *our*.

He said, "Maybe the sword didn't call you. Maybe it's just dumb luck. But destiny is always looking backward, so who can tell? Regardless of whether you were chosen or stumbled into it, you can feel it now. Your white-knuckled grip says as much."

"It feels right," I said.

"It always does. You can carry it for now. I don't need it."

With that, the sword felt lighter in my hands. It wasn't a done deal. There was some connection to this man of light. I couldn't describe it other than a bond between me, him, and the sword. The three of us tied together in an invisible knot.

"I'm Monty," he said.

"Ortiz."

"Walk with me."

We walked toward the ridge. We weren't that far out of town, but this road led nowhere in particular, so there wasn't much traffic at this time of night.

"You are now a man of purpose," he said. "The universe has given you a responsibility."

"That seems like a bad idea."

"Nobody said the universe was smart."

My car was parked nearby. I searched my pockets for the keys, only now remembering that they were in Roger's pockets. And Roger was in the bottom of a bottomless pit. It was discouraging, but considering how my night could have gone, I tried to look on the bright side.

"So this is a magic sword?" I asked.

"Magic is too small a word for what that sword is." He leaned against the car. "But, sure, if that's how you want to think of it. Though what power it has is locked away until it's put in the right hands."

"Who?"

"Whose," he corrected. "I'm hungry. Been ages since I've eaten. Longer. Do they still have food?"

"Yes," I said. "Food still exists."

"Ah, good. Let's get some, then."

"I don't have my keys."

"Try the door. Maybe your friend forgot to lock his side."

I pulled the handle, and the door opened. I could've sworn I saw Roger lock it, but maybe not.

I put the sword in the back seat. I debated whether it was safer to put the pointy side up or down, deciding to lay it across the floorboard. After we climbed into the car, I said, "Still don't have the keys."

"Try the visor."

I pulled down the visor. Keys fell into my lap.

"But I saw him take these and put them in his pocket," I said.

"Did you." He nodded toward the road. "Drive."

The road eventually hit the freeway and from there it was only a short drive to the edge of town. I had questions, but I didn't ask them. I was alive. I allowed myself to enjoy that for a while.

I found a Denny's. Monty's appearance might freak out the staff, but I was more worried about the sword. I hadn't even realized I'd carried it inside until the hostess came to greet us. Grabbing it had just been a reflex.

There are TV shows and movies where people are able to walk around with swords by hiding them under long coats or behind their back or some bullshit like that. This, unsurprisingly, was not possible for me. I didn't have a long coat, and even if I had, it wouldn't have worked.

The woman looked at us, a shining sun in a dusty suit and a guy covered in dirt, carrying a sword.

"Table or booth?"

"Surprise us," said Monty.

The woman smiled politely, but also with cold eyes that said she was not genuinely amused. Soon we were sitting at a booth, perusing the menu while the server got our drinks. I sat the sword beside me, point up to keep from poking holes in the Naugahyde that had a few holes already. But saw no reason to be impolite and add one more.

"Who buried this?" I asked.

"It wasn't buried. It was thrown into the Gorge, along with myself. The hope was that we would be gone forever, but here we are. Oh, I see that they're still making pancakes. Can't beat the classics. Strawberry or banana?"

"What?"

"What's your preference?"

"I like blueberry."

He stuck out his glittering tongue. "Hard to believe the universe would trust you as a bearer, but who am I to question it?"

The server returned, took our orders. After she was gone, Monty said, "Why isn't she making a big deal about the sword? That's what you're wondering, right?"

"Had crossed my mind."

"Most people live in the Waking World. They see what they want to see, what they're ready to see. She's not ready."

"So I'm not supposed to give the sword to her?" I asked.

"Do you want to give it to her?"

"No."

"Well, then you shouldn't give it to her."

"But I could, if I wanted to?"

"It's your boon to offer. You can give it to whomever you want." He took a sip of his Diet Coke. I half expected the beverage to splash through his hologram head. "Every bearer sets their own standards."

"There are others?"

"Other boons, and other bearers to carry them," he said. "They like to view themselves as wise guardians of sacred powers. They see humanity as beneath them, forgetting that all of us started out human. Underneath it all, underneath this"—he waved a hand over his rainbow face—"we still are. That's their sin. Forgetting that."

He leaned forward, and his eyes burned brighter.

"But I never did. And when I sought to become more, to truly rise to become a god as they pretended to be, as they betrayed me for it."

Something passed through us. A tidal wave of hate and rage and bitterness and sadness that rose out of Monty and washed over me through our link.

"Those sons of bitches," I said, not knowing who I was talking about but feeling it deeper than my bones. Then the sensation drained from me as Monty cracked a smile.

"It's fine," he said. "I'm over it. I really am. They did me a favor. They don't know it yet, but they will."

Silence filled the space as Monty drank his coffee. He didn't ask about me, and why would he? I wasn't an interesting guy. Even I wasn't interested in me.

As for Monty, I had questions, but I didn't ask them. Some part of me knew I wouldn't ask the right ones, and if I did, I wouldn't like the answers. I'd survived this long by keeping my head down. Curiosity was a luxury for other people. Better to appreciate that I was still alive because of a magic sword and keep my mouth shut.

The server came over with our food. Monty poured syrup on his tall stack of pancakes. When I was foolish enough to dare to ask another question, he held up a hand.

"Can't talk. Eating."

We ate instead of talking, and my BLT tasted pretty good, considering I could've been dead. After he pushed away his plate, he continued.

"Now let's talk about you, and your new position of importance. As the sword-bearer, you are now part of the Dreaming World, which is the real world. Not that the Waking World isn't real. But the Dreaming World is more real."

"Seems like it should be the opposite," I said.

He cracked a smile. "The Waking World is the top five percent of reality as you know it. The Dreaming part is the other ninety-five percent. It's like our own minds. We imagine ourselves doing the thinking, but all the hard work is being done in the unconscious. Our behavior is more an expression of those unconscious processes than anything we deliberately choose."

"I guess."

"Never mind. Understanding isn't important. It's probably not even possible. All you really need to know is that you are now a chosen child of the universe." He held out his hand. "Let me see your wallet."

He pulled out all the cash and credit cards. His hand flared brighter and burned the money to ash and melted the cards into a plastic lump. When I tried to say something, he just winked at me.

"Have any other money on you?"

"No."

"Great. Let's pay the bill now."

He walked up to our server at the cashier. "It's on him." He handed me my empty wallet, aside from a sandwich club frequent buyer card.

The server gave me the check as I absently reached into my pocket, but I had nothing. I was about to explain that when I spotted something under my dirty sneaker. I moved my foot aside to see several folded bills. I handed it to the cashier.

"The question you're asking is was that always there or did the universe conjure it up just now," said Monty. "The answer is that it doesn't matter. The Dreaming World is more flexible, and its flexibility now works in your favor. And this is where we part ways for now. *Buena suerte*, Ortiz."

"I don't speak Spanish," I said.

That amused him. "It means good luck." He stepped outside with a nod and smile.

The cashier tried to give me back my change, but I waved it away. It wasn't my money. Or maybe it was, but I figured she was having a bad day of her own, so why not share my fortune.

Outside, Monty was gone.

I stood there, holding the sword. I didn't understand much of it, but the world, Waking or Dreaming or whatever, was on my side for once. It was too good to be true, but maybe I was due some good luck.

I stepped off the curb. It was my fault that I wasn't paying attention, even if the car was going way too fast for a parking lot. The headlights blinded me for a moment before the car hit a pothole, bouncing to one side, colliding with a lamppost, hitting hard enough to put a sizable dent and trigger the airbags.

The passenger door opened, and a big guy fell out, stumbling around on shaky legs. Blood trickled down his nostril. His nose might have been broken. Or maybe it was just like that.

"What the fuck is wrong with you?" he slurred.

"Sorry," I said.

He didn't take the apology in the spirit it was offered, and if he could see the sword, he didn't care. He reached for me with his meaty hands.

A truck plowed into him, missing me by inches. The guy was launched a dozen feet as the truck came to a screeching stop. Its driver stuck his head out the window.

"Oh, shit, dude." He looked at the crumpled guy, then at me. "Shit, dude. Are you okay?"

"Yeah, I'm good." I pulled the sword closer, holding it in two hands. "I'm great."

CHAPTER TWO

The next morning, I awoke with the sword leaning against the *Masters of the Universe* TV tray that served as my bedside table. Yesterday had been rough, but today, I had my sword.

I took a shower, washing away the last of the dirt from what was supposed to be my own grave. Then I dug the old golf bag out of the back of my closet. It'd been there when I'd moved into the apartment. No clubs. Just the bag. At the time, I hadn't thought much about it, but now, as I shoved the sword into it, I considered that maybe it had been a sign sent by the universe.

Probably not.

With the bag slung over my shoulder and a song in my heart, I set out to fix my fucked-up life. I didn't expect it to go smoothly, even with the universe on my side, but I hit a snag sooner than expected.

Opening my front door, the hallway was gone. A small room was in its place. A lonely little chair sat in the lonely little room. There wasn't much to the chair at a glance. Aside from some intricate runic carvings in the wood, it wouldn't have been out of place pushed up against a folding table.

The chair stood before me, daring me to sit in it. I'd never been challenged by a piece of furniture before, but there was no mistaking the aura of disdain. It was more than a general contempt. The chair didn't like me, specifically.

I closed the door and opened it again. The little room was gone. The hall was back, along with a bag of groceries. I picked it up and placed it two doors down. The sound of a TV blaring came from within, so I knocked hard.

"Mrs. Cuervo, I got your groceries again!" I shouted.

I often left it at that, but the TV volume didn't change. I knocked once more, figured I'd done my due diligence, and started to walk away.

The door opened a crack. Mrs. Cuervo, her face full of wrinkles and one white eye, sucked on her dentures.

"It's Ms. Cuervo," she said.

"Oh, yeah. Sorry. They delivered your groceries to me." I gestured toward the bag. It was a lot more Ensure, Polident, and lottery tickets than I generally kept stocked.

"They do it on purpose," she said.

"Maybe you have the wrong apartment number in the app," I said.

She fixed me with her good eye. "Are you saying I don't know my own apartment number?"

I slinked backward with a shrug. "Maybe you put it in wrong."

She grabbed the bag with a withered hand, dragged it into the darkened apartment. "I know my own goddamn apartment number."

"Yeah." I found myself staring into her dead eye. "Apps, right? They're pretty stupid."

She snorted and nodded to me. It wasn't approval. More like tolerance. "What's with the golf bag? You golfing now? Golfing is a stupid thing to do."

"They say it's good exercise." I didn't know why I responded other than a mild attempt to defend myself. "But I'm not golfing. It's just an old bag I found."

"It's bad for the environment. Not that it matters much to me. I'm going to be dead soon, thank god. Never got the groceries delivered wrong when we used phones." Ms. Cuervo sucked on her teeth again. "You know what I mean."

"Sure." I turned toward the stairs. "Technology."

The neutral statement satisfied her, and she retreated into her sanctuary. The TV was back to blasting by the time I descended to the building's broken-down lobby.

Outside, I took a moment to enjoy the fresh air and sunshine. Except the air smelled like burning rubber, and a pair of skyscrapers cast cold shadows over my block. Still, it felt like a brand-new day.

"Looking good, Mr. Ortiz," said Rachel from her usual perch leaning against the apartment building.

The neighborhood had an ever-shifting homeless population. Rachel and her boyfriend had stuck around longer than most. Homelessness made people into inconvenient objects to be ignored. I'd have liked to think myself more empathetic, but I did my share of ignoring. It was just easier, lousy as that was to say.

But there was something about these two kids. In another time, another world, they'd have been starting their way toward hopes and dreams. Now they just lived day by day.

I'd never asked their story. It didn't make much difference. Whether their own foolish choices or bad luck, who was I to judge?

Rachel approached. I'd never learned her boyfriend's name. Never spoken to him. I got the feeling that life had used him up a long time ago, and she would have been better off without him. But it wasn't my place to say.

"Hey, hate to bother you, Mr. Ortiz." She stuffed her hands in her pockets. "But you got any spare change?"

I checked my pockets, only to remember that Monty had destroyed all my money. But I was a bearer. I had the universe on my side. Surely, I could find some.

I looked around to see if I was standing on any loose bills. I checked my pockets again. Nothing came up.

"Sorry, kid," I said. "I'll have to get you later."

She had a sweet smile. There was a desperation in it, hanging onto the edge by her fingernails. "No problem, Mr. Ortiz. Hey, that's a nice bag. I didn't know you golfed. My dad golfed. Good exercise, right?"

"So I've heard," I replied.

She returned to her boyfriend's side. They huddled against the wall, trying to make themselves as small as possible. Even in this neighborhood, it wasn't unusual for a passing cop, if they were bored enough, to hassle the kids.

"Hey, Rachel," I said. "Do you like SpaghettiOs? I have a couple of cans I'm not going to eat."

She nodded. "Yeah. SpaghettiOs are cool."

I turned to go upstairs to retrieve them when I ran smack-dab into Dwayne and Bill.

Dwayne was tall and wide. Bill was short and wide. The fact they were both wide threw off their dynamic. Dwayne was the smart one, and he wasn't very smart.

"Hey, guys," I said. "I was just getting something for the kids and then some breakfast and then heading over to talk to the boss."

Dwayne glowered. "Where's Roger?"

"He's dead." I would've been more delicate with the news, but Dwayne and Roger had never gotten along. "A tree fell on him."

Bill said, "That supposed to be funny or something?"

I replied, "It was a little bit funny, though you really had to be there."

Dwayne put a hand on my shoulder. "You're coming with us."

"I wouldn't do that," I said. "I could really use some french toast. I promise I'll talk to Horace after."

Dwayne and Bill flanked me. I expected the universe to flatten them in some unexpected way. Maybe a couple of safes falling from above like a classic cartoon.

"Okay, fine. But can I get the SpaghettiOs first?" I said.

"Everything okay, Mr. Ortiz?" asked Rachel.

"Nothing to worry about, kids."

The universe stood by as the goons hustled me into the back seat of their car.

"Sorry about this," I told her. "I'll be back in a bit."

Bill slammed the door shut, and then we were down the street.

"You could've at least let me feed them."

"Fuck 'em," said Dwayne.

"They're just kids," said Bill.

"They should get jobs."

"It's not that easy," said Bill.

Dwayne grunted. "Whatever."

They hadn't taken my bag. They hadn't even searched it. Some people weren't ready to see the sword, and I guess the bag didn't change that.

Monty had also said that I was protected while I carried the sword, but Dwayne and Bill had definitely laid hands on me. They hadn't tried to kill me, though. Or even hurt me. That must have been the difference.

Roger was going to shoot me with clear ill-intent. The driver last night wasn't trying to hit me, but if he had, it would've done some damage. His attempt to punch me after was an obvious threat of physical harm. Bill and Dwayne just wanted to take me to Horace, where I was planning to go anyway. This was a little ahead of schedule, but that was more of an inconvenience than anything else.

Dwayne studied me from the rearview mirror. “Roger was always a goddamn idiot. Didn’t think he was stupid enough for you to get the drop on him, though.”

Bill laughed. “Ortiz getting the drop on anybody is a fucking joke.”

The drive passed without further conversation.

We pulled up to the boss’s estate. They nodded to the guards at the gate, who nodded back, letting us in. Then we drove up to the wide, three-story house. I’d never counted the rooms, but I knew there were too many. Nobody needed that many rooms. They started doing weird things with them, like decorating them in an individual theme and purpose.

Horace MacDonald’s house had a billiard room and a poker room and a home theater and a sauna and a dining room and a working tavern with imported beer on tap and a wine cellar and a breakfast nook. It was all paid for with blood money. None of that blood was his.

I hadn’t seen all the rooms, but I’d been to the downstairs guest bathroom. It was an ugly little box with mismatched tile, cheap fixtures, and no personality. It was the room he had for the help, who he wasn’t trying to impress, and it said everything about him. The ballroom was who he wanted to be, but his soul was a leaky toilet in a dingy room with single-ply toilet paper.

Dwayne and Bill led me into the nook, where Horace sat at a small table in the warm late-morning light. He was always impeccably dressed. Wrinkle-free button-up shirt, neatly creased slacks. His haircut was so precise, I was convinced he had it trimmed once an hour to make sure not a single hair was out of place. He gestured toward the seat across from him where a plate of french toast waited for me.

Well played, Universe.

I draped my golf bag across the back of the chair and had a seat. I poured some syrup over my breakfast. Nobody said anything as I spread the butter and took a bite.

“Man, that’s good,” I said.

"I'll give your regards to the chef," said Horace without a smile.

Horace didn't smile often. Maybe when he got to watch someone get kneecapped.

"What's with the bag?" he asked.

"It carries my sword," I said. "For now. I'll pick up something better soon."

He snapped his fingers and a butler poured him some orange juice. He could've done it himself. The pitcher was right there within reach. But Horace liked making people do things.

"Where did you get a sword?"

"Long story," I replied, pouring my own juice. "Fresh squeezed?"

The butler nodded.

"Can I see it?" asked Horace. "The sword?"

I pulled the weapon halfway out of the bag. He reached for it, but I shook my head. I said, "You see with your eyes. Not your hands."

He wasn't used to being told no, but he didn't push it. Maybe he sensed that getting between me and the sword was a mistake. Maybe he assumed he'd get a better look once I was dead.

"Irene around?" I asked.

"She's out at some thing," said Horace. "Some aerobics thing."

"Hot yoga," said Bill.

Horace glared. "Whatever. I thought it'd be better if she weren't around when we had this talk. She know about the money?"

"Funny," I said. "I was going to ask you the same thing."

He said, "You can tell me the truth. I'm not going to do anything to her if she was in on it. She's a real pain in my ass, but even I wouldn't kill her for what you two skimmed."

"You could always cut off a finger or two," said Dwayne.

Horace snarled, but Dwayne was not deterred.

"Just a pinkie. Might teach her some respect."

"I don't remember asking you for your opinion," said Horace.

Dwayne opened his mouth, but Bill pulled him back. "He doesn't mean anything by it. He just hates seeing you being treated that way when you've always been so good to her."

Horace grumbled. He turned his attention back to me.

"I've gotten where I am by knowing people. Specifically, I know about guts. Guys who have guts can be a problem. Guys with guts have dreams and ambitions. I'd have never picked you as a guy with guts."

"I'm as surprised as you," I replied.

He almost smiled.

I'd survived as long as I had working for Horace by being mildly useful. I did little things that needed doing. Nothing important. You'd have to be an idiot to trust me with a gun. But I'd done all right by running errands that needed a reliable stooge who was disposable enough to be a fall guy if things went south. I was a mascot of the operation, but I was as surprised as anyone that I'd lasted this long.

I'd seen plenty of people come and go working for Horace. They usually left feetfirst, though some were lucky enough to limp away with only a few broken bones and missing teeth. Nobody walked away without scars. Staying came with scars, too. That was how it worked with Horace.

My secret had been keeping my head down. Don't make friends. Don't make enemies. Do the job. Keep my mouth shut. It had worked until she'd come along.

"I have a rule," said Horace. "I leave the unpleasant tasks to other guys. Some asshole gets shot in the head? I'm across town at a dinner party. Some idiot watches their business go up in smoke? I'm tucked in bed, dreaming pleasant dreams."

He folded his hands.

"But sometimes, I consider making an exception."

He expected me to beg for my life. Why else drag me here when he was just going to have Dwayne or Bill kill me? He was smart enough not to pull the trigger himself, but he missed that part of it. He loved the idea of holding someone's life in his fist and squeezing.

Some part of me sat on edge, of course. Sword or not, blessed or not, it was human nature. I couldn't change that; but also, I'd been preparing for this meeting a while now. I'd never expected to get away with any of it. I wasn't the guy who got away with stuff.

I'd resolved that I wouldn't give him the satisfaction, and I didn't know if I would've kept that promise without the sword. But I had the sword.

"Horace, you're a real piece of shit. You know that, right?"

God, it felt great to say. Felt even better to say it before taking a bite of his french toast at his own table.

Dwayne put a hand on me, but before he could incur the wrath of the universe, Horace waved him off.

"You think it's guts?" I laughed. "You don't have to be afraid of the guy with guts and ambition. You can always pull their strings, threaten the things they love, offer them promises. But a guy with nothing, a guy like me, that's the guy who's going to put a bullet in you one day."

He frowned. The rage boiled just underneath his calm.

"You act like you're a tough guy," I said. "But you're neutered. You might have been dangerous once, but now you're just a dumbass who postures while other people get their hands dirty. People like Dwayne and Bill and me, we're out there risking our necks while an asshole like you sits in houses like this and acts like you're King Shit. Well, you're not tough. You're just a guy with a breakfast nook."

Horace said nothing. He stewed in his silent anger.

"Lucky for you," I said, "I'm not a guy with nothing. I've got my sword. And I don't have anything against you. Not really. And I don't need the money anymore. I haven't spent any of it. I'll give it all back, and we'll call it even. But fuck with me and I can't be responsible for what happens."

I took my last bite of french toast and flashed a condescending smile. After a lifetime of being the least important person in the room, it felt glorious.

Horace clutched a butter knife in his fist. Hate seethed in his eyes. It'd been a long time since anyone had dared talk to him like this. He'd outsourced the unpleasant business to others, but that anger had never gone away. Maybe it had gotten worse with no way to vent it. He wanted nothing more than to drive that knife into my throat, and I wanted him to try. I'd liked Roger, but if the sword sucked Horace into a deep, deep hole, it would only be an improvement for the universe.

Dwayne stepped up. "We'll get him to take us to the money stash."

Horace reluctantly set down the knife. "Get him the fuck out of my sight."

I slung the golf bag over my shoulder, finished off my juice. "All right, boys. Let's do it."

Back in the car, I gave Dwayne and Bill directions to the place I'd hidden the skimmed money. A few hundred here and there. I'd hoped it would add up fast enough to get me out of town before anyone noticed, but it'd always been a long shot.

Three blocks from my apartment was a broken-down building. It'd been long abandoned. Sometimes, a sign would go up, promising an exciting new real estate development, but the sign always went away. It was three stories of broken windows and graffiti, a yawning money pit that so far had devoured anyone stupid enough to try and make it into anything.

Inside, the building had been gutted. You might find rats or homeless people inside. Addicts might be there, but they weren't dangerous. People who ended up in the building were used to being ignored and forgotten, so they returned the favor.

Dwayne and Bill shuffled dutifully behind me. "Jesus, Ortiz, this is a hell of a place," said Bill.

"You'd never think to look here," I said.

In a corner, I pulled back the decaying drywall to reveal the duffle bag of cash. I stepped aside, but Dwayne and Bill were reluctant to stick their hands in the dark crevice.

"Allow me." I pulled out the bag and placed it on the ground before me. "It's all there. You can count it."

"We'll count it later." Dwayne pulled out a knife. A big one.

"Ah, shit," said Bill. "Not the knife. Can't we just shoot him?"

"Someone could hear a gunshot."

"Yeah, but the knife, it's so messy."

"Why do you care? I'm the one who's going to do it."

"What happens when you get some on you? Then I gotta smell blood the whole car ride back."

"I won't get blood on me."

"Like hell. You always get blood on you."

Dwayne groaned. "Fine. You want to shoot him, then? You shoot him." He put the knife away and grabbed the duffle bag. "But the boss said to make him suffer."

"Who cares?" Bill drew his gun. "The boss isn't here. We'll tell him he screamed like a little bitch. Begged for his life. The boss just wants a good story. So we'll give him one."

He pointed the gun at me.

"You don't want to do that," I said.

They chuckled.

Pieces of the rotted ceiling fell down on their heads. Nothing serious enough to hurt, but enough to get their attention. Bill lowered the gun, and the building stopped its attack.

"That's a warning from the universe," I said. "You probably won't get another. Just take the money and go. Give Horace a good story. I promise you won't see me again."

Bill took aim again. The reaction was swift. The floor fell out from under him, and he plummeted into the darkness below. I hadn't even known the building had a basement.

"How did you do that?" asked Dwayne.

"Sword," I replied. He wouldn't have bought a deeper explanation.

He pulled out his knife. You'd think after Roger and now Bill that he'd maybe reconsider me as a threat, but why should he? I'd never been a threat to anyone before yesterday.

He took a step toward me, and the ceiling caved in, burying him under tons of rubble and—I kid you not—a giant old-timey safe. I lost sight of him under all that, but I imagined him flattened like a pancake. They'd dig him out and stick an air pump in his mouth and he'd be fine.

I considered the money. I could take it back to Horace, but that'd just lead to more carnage. The universe was on my side, but that didn't mean I needed to use it as a weapon. I didn't want anyone hurt. Not Roger. Not Dwayne. Not Bill. Not even Horace.

I didn't need the money now, but money was nice.

"That's a nice golf bag," said someone.

Rachel and her boyfriend stepped from the shadows.

"Jesus, kids," I said. "You scared me."

Rachel smiled. There was no warmth in it. Only hunger. She licked her lips.

"Can I have it, Mr. Ortiz?" She moved closer, and the building shook.

"You don't want this," I said.

She held out her hand. "Give it to us."

"Give it to me!" shouted her boyfriend. It was the first words I'd ever heard him speak.

She shoved him aside. "No. It's mine! I'm his friend."

He lurched past her, only a few grasping steps from me. "I need it more than her!"

Part of the ceiling collapsed. He jumped back as a chunk nearly struck him. The warning didn't faze him as he took a step around the debris. I outweighed him by about fifty pounds, but his scrawny arms were knotted. The veins on his neck bulged. His bloodshot eyes never strayed from the golf bag. It made it easier for Rachel to bash his head in with a brick.

He fell prostrate. His cracked skull spilled a pool of blood. He twitched with one eye on the golf bag as he dragged himself across the dirty floor.

Rachel stepped over him. He grabbed her ankle. She kicked him in the face.

"Give me the fucking bag!" she screamed, still clutching the bloody brick. I didn't doubt for a minute that she'd use it against me.

"You can have some of the money," I said, kicking it toward her. "You can have all of it."

She looked at the duffle bag. Clarity fell across her. She dropped the brick, saw her boyfriend gagging to death in his own blood.

"Oh, god. Oh, god. Oh, Blair, baby, I'm so sorry. I'm so sorry."

"It'll be okay," I said. "You're okay now. We'll call an ambulance, and—"

Rachel fixed me with a hard stare. No, not me. The golf bag. The hunger was back in her eyes.

"You have to get control of yourself," I said, but it was clear that control wasn't an option. Whatever had her wasn't going to let go again.

The building trembled. Cracks ran along the ceiling as drywall dust fell on our heads.

"We have to get out of here," I said.

"Just give me the bag," said Rachel. "You can have the money. I don't care about the fucking money." She grabbed the duffle and threw it at my feet.

I tossed the money over my shoulder while clutching the golf bag tighter. The tremors rattled everything. The wall behind me collapsed. Light filtered through the hole left behind, offering me an escape route.

"Don't do it," she said. "Don't—"

I bolted but only made it a few steps before she was on me. She must've weighed all of a hundred pounds, but she tackled me with surprising force. She tried to yank the golf bag off my back, but the straps were wrapped around me. I couldn't get my feet under me as she dragged me across the floor.

"Give it to me!" She screeched like an animal. She snatched up a piece of loose rebar and raised it to cave in my face.

Then the entire building fell down on both our heads.

CHAPTER THREE

I used my phone's flashlight to see why I wasn't dead.

All that debris, several tons of rubble, had entangled itself in a lattice over my head. It was like pushing over a house of cards and having all the cards line up just right.

Rachel's hand stuck out from the rubble. I tugged the golf bag loose, but her dead fingers were wrapped tight. It took a minute to break them free, one at a time. After, her hand was still like a grasping claw.

A piece of the delicately balanced roof fell off at my feet. Even the will of the universe itself couldn't defy odds forever. I followed the tunnel outside. The moment I stepped onto the street, the tunnel collapsed behind me. Only half the building had fallen, but the half still standing didn't look so good.

A couple walking a dog came up to me. "Hey, man, are you all right?" asked the man.

"I'm fine," I said.

"Was anyone else in there?"

"Three or four. They might still be alive."

But they weren't. The universe had made sure of that. I didn't feel bad about Bill and Dwayne. They were bad guys. But Rachel and her boyfriend hadn't deserved this. Whatever had taken control of them, it had transformed two kids into monsters.

It had to be the sword. Nothing else it could be. I could've taken precautions. I could've done something to keep this from happening. But Monty hadn't warned me.

"It's not my fault," I said. "I didn't ask the universe to do that."

"You're in shock," said the man. "Someone needs to take a look at you."

"I'm okay."

I was covered in a light smattering of dust, but there wasn't a scratch on me. It was preposterous from their perspective.

It was pretty fucking preposterous from mine.

To them, I was just a person walking away from disaster, but I knew better. I was the disaster.

The guy reached for me, but I pulled away. I expected a meteor to come screaming out of the blue sky and flatten the poor bastard. It didn't happen. Yet.

I didn't understand these rules. Dwayne and Bill had been able to kidnap me, but maybe that was because I hadn't really cared if they had. Or maybe it was because they weren't a direct danger at that moment. Maybe the universe only resorted to deadly force when warranted.

But what about Rachel and Blair. They'd been possessed by something, driven to dangerous madness, but there had to be an easier way for the universe to stop them than dropping a building on them.

I needed to get off the street.

"I'm fine," I said in a mild panic, clutching my golf bag and duffle close as I ran back to my apartment. It was only a couple of blocks. Nobody followed me. Back inside my place, I slammed the door and tossed the bags on the floor.

I'd always been a loser, and a loser working for Horace was always going to end up dead. I'd never expected to get away with the money, but if I was going to die at least I'd die doing something optimistically stupid. That was the way it had been headed until the sword came along. But the sword had come along, and now it looked my like my rotten luck had been exported to those around me. I wouldn't have wished that on anybody.

"Ortiz?" said Irene's voice from my bedroom. "Is that you?"

I didn't need this now.

"Ortiz?" she said.

I cleared my head and went to the bedroom. Irene sat on the edge of my bed. She jumped up and moved to hug me but stopped when she saw the white dust on me.

"Jesus, are you hurt?" she asked.

"I'm fine," I replied. "Building just fell on me. That's all."

"Oh my god," she said. "That's what that sound was?"

Irene was not the girl of my dreams. Like most things in my life, she was a product of making the best of what came along. She was pretty, but not too pretty. She was funny, but not too funny. She was good in bed, but not great in bed.

No doubt she would've said all the same things about me. We were in like, not love.

Irene was Horace MacDonald's only daughter. Stepdaughter, in fact. Her mother had died young, shortly in the marriage. A smart move. Had she lived, Horace no doubt would've rubbed her the wrong way. But by checking out early, she'd left him with a memory he couldn't fuck up.

Horace smiled when he thought about hurting someone. And when he talked about Irene's mom. And that was it.

Those memories kept Irene in his good graces. They fought. A lot. She didn't like him. He didn't like her, but he took care of her.

She wiped dust off my shoulders and chest then hugged me delicately. She rubbed the dust off my chin and kissed me. "I'm just glad you're alive. He thinks you stole some money from him. I told him there's no way you'd do that."

I took off my shirt, letting the dust fall on my brown carpet. I hadn't vacuumed ever so it wasn't that big a deal. "I took the money."

"You what?"

"I stole it." I grabbed a shirt off the floor and sniffed it. It was a little musty, but most everything I owned was piled in the laundry bin in my bathroom.

"Are you fucking crazy? Why would you do that?"

"I stole it for us," I said.

"Us? We don't need money."

I put the shirt on. "No, you don't need money. Except you do. Because all your money is Horace's money."

"He doesn't own me."

"So if I'd asked you to run away with me, to leave this town with nothing in our pockets and never look back, you'd have said yes?"

"Oh, now you're just being dumb."

It wasn't a yes, but I didn't push it.

"Horace has more money than he needs," I said. "I needed it. I was hoping we'd skip town before he noticed."

"Well, he noticed."

I sat on the bed. "I noticed."

She sat beside me, took my hand. "You stupid bastard, you didn't have to do that for me."

"I didn't do it just for you. I saw an opportunity, and I took it."

"How much did you take?" she asked.

"Enough that he noticed. Enough for us to get by for a while. It's in the bag by the door."

"I'll talk to him. Get him to change his mind."

"Yes, Horace is well known for his forgiving nature."

I'd stolen from him, killed three of his goons, and, worst of all, mouthed off to him in his very own breakfast nook. If the world ended tomorrow, and Horace and I were the last two people left, he'd have strangled me in the ruins.

"Since when do you golf?"

I yanked the golf bag out of her reach. I didn't know if the sword cared if she touched it, but I felt bad enough about the people the universe had hurt on my behalf already. I didn't need Irene on that list.

I threw the bag over my shoulder as she gave me a funny look. "I was just thinking about pawning this old thing."

I stared deep into her eyes to see if there was any trace of that hunger that had taken control of Rachel and Blair. I didn't see anything, but I hadn't seen it in them at first.

"Yeah, I'll probably just throw it out."

She turned her attention to the duffle bag, unzipped it, and withdrew a stack of cash. "Do you have any cigarettes?"

"I thought you were quitting."

She threw the wad hard into my chest, but it was only paper. "I was, but then the guy I was screwing stole money from my psychotic stepfather. So I think I can have a fucking cigarette if I want a fucking cigarette." She rifled through my sock drawer, and found an open pack. "Oh, thank god."

"You hid cigarettes in my apartment?"

"Hid?" She laughed. "You saw me put these here. Promised me you'd throw them out after I left. Fortunately for me you're a lousy housekeeper."

She pushed her way past me. In the kitchenette she paused at the electric stove.

"Ah, damn it. I forgot. You don't have a lighter, do you."

"Check the junk drawer."

A search of its mismatched contents turned up three lighters. Two didn't work, but she fought the third until it gave up a flame. She tossed the lighters back into the drawer as she sucked in a lungful of nicotine.

"Okay, so what do we do now?"

I smiled.

"What are you grinning about, dumbass?" she asked.

"So we're a *we*?"

She glared. "Don't make a big thing about it. I like you, Jay."

"I like you, too."

She blew clouds toward my smoke detector, but it didn't have any batteries. Never had.

"We both know that the worst that Horace will do to me is scream at me for hooking up with a moron. He won't be wrong. But I don't want you dead. You've gotta leave town. Don't tell anyone where you're going. Don't even tell me. Shit, you should've already left town. It's too late."

"No, it's not," I said. "I've got a plan."

"You've got a plan?"

"You don't have to sound so surprised."

"Oh, I'm not surprised. I'm worried. You're not so great with plans."

"I'm okay with plans."

"Your last plan involved stealing money from Horace."

"That's just stage one," I said.

"What's stage two? Digging your own grave before someone gutshoots you?"

"I thought so, yeah, but things have turned around."

"Okay. So what's the plan?"

"I'm still working on it."

"See, that doesn't fill me with confidence."

"It's cool. I have enough confidence for both of us."

I kissed her. She tasted of ash and like. My hands went down her back. She pushed me away.

"Tell me you're not trying to get lucky now."

I shrugged.

She brushed some of the dust that had fallen in her hair and down her shirt. "Unbelievable."

I guided her toward the front door. "Just go home. Act like nothing's wrong. You didn't know about the money before. So just keep acting like you don't know. I can straighten this out, but I need you to stay away from me. It's too dangerous to be around me right now."

She stabbed out her cigarette on the kitchen counter. "No shit."

I opened the door and gently pushed her out, but she grabbed me by the arm. "Ortiz, a lot of guys came and went with Horace. And I could've slept with most of them, but I didn't because they were all assholes and morons. So then along comes a guy who's only a moron . . ."

She put a hand on my face.

"Just don't die on me, dumbass."

I pressed her palm to my lips. I didn't say anything. Saying something would just screw it up. If things went south, if the sword wasn't enough, I wanted to remember her face. Her sweet smile. Her disapproving furrowed brow. It summarized our relationship better than any words could.

I closed the door.

"And hide the money, you idiot!" she shouted from the other side.

CHAPTER FOUR

My list of problems didn't seem smaller than they had been yesterday, despite the sword. I wasn't too worried about Horace, but what had happened to Rachel and Blair lurked in my concerns.

They'd been possessed by something, and that something had taken a couple of sweet kids and turned them into violent killers. If the universe hadn't dropped a building on them, Rachel would've caved in my skull to get her hands on my sword.

Most people didn't seem to care about the sword, but I couldn't walk the streets with something that could transform ordinary people into dangerous psychos. I'd already caused the death of Rachel and Blair. Sure, I'd also been responsible, in a roundabout way, for the deaths of Roger and Bill and Dwayne. But they were all lousy guys. I sort of liked Roger, but he still had done a lot of bad stuff for Horace. Live by the sword, die by the tree.

Rachel and her boyfriend were different. If I'd never found this sword, if I'd died in that hole the way I was supposed to, they'd still be alive. I hadn't pulled the trigger. I hadn't even asked the universe to do anything. But I was responsible.

I could still see her hungry eyes, that confusion on her face after she'd brained Blair, only to have that confusion disappear a moment later in her desire for the sword.

My plan last night had been a simple one. Get the money. Get Irene. Get out of town. Ride off into a bright future with the universe on my side.

Now I kept coming back to the question. How long could Irene be exposed to the sword before that same look burned in her eyes?

I thought with the boon that I couldn't lose, and maybe I couldn't. But I could cause a lot of damage. So here I was, trapped in my apartment, with a bunch of questions and no answers.

I took the sword out of the golf bag and set it on my kitchen table. It didn't look like much. I felt a connection to it, impossible to quantify. Like rediscovering a favorite toy I had as a child that I'd forgotten about. There was an intimacy. It was just a sword, but it was my sword.

Mine to hold. Mine to give.

I could leave it here. That might be safer. If no one saw it, no one could want it, right? There were risks. Its protection might have a range limit. Unguarded, it might be vulnerable to being stolen. I didn't know the rules well enough.

I took the sword, wrapped it in a towel, and wrapped that in duct tape. I put that in the golf bag for an extra layer of protection. In the back of my closet, there was an old access panel where I'd hidden the money for a while before moving it to the old building. I unscrewed the panel, shoved the golf bag in, and screwed the panel shut. For good measure, I threw a pile of dirty laundry in front of it. It wasn't likely to fool anyone who came looking, but like a guy stuffing his keys way down in his shoes at the beach, it was the best option I had.

A tingle ran through me as I stepped away from the closet. I could feel the sword, hiding behind the wall. It didn't like it there. It wanted to be by my side, but I pushed aside the twitch. I grabbed a glass of water, sat at my kitchen table, closed my eyes, and let the feeling pass.

It took a few minutes.

I opened my eyes as the tension faded. Maybe I could manage this.

The sword sat in the chair beside me.

"Son of a bitch."

In an experimental mood, I went to the apartment hall, closing the door behind me. The pull hit me again. When it finally faded, I found the sword had followed me outside again, sitting at my feet.

Couldn't ditch the thing even if I wanted to.

I took it back inside, got the golf bag out of the closet, and wrapped the towel around the sword and shoved it back in the bag.

"Look," I said. "I don't know if you're alive or aware or whatever, but we have to make this work. For the both of us."

The sword said nothing. I didn't expect it to, but if it could level a building, it should've been able to give me a sign.

Someone knocked on the front door.

I opened the door a crack. A slim woman with blue skin and long, long green hair stood in the hallway. She wore flower print bell-bottoms and a frilly shirt that fell off one shoulder. Her eyes were bottomless cerulean pools.

"Where's the goddamn sword?" she asked as she pushed the door, shoving me aside easily.

"What sword?" I replied.

She glowered and strode toward the golf bag.

"Don't touch that!" I grabbed her by the arm, and she stopped. But it wasn't because of me.

She glared at my hand. "Do you mind?"

I released her. "Just don't touch the bag."

"I'm not an idiot," she said.

I studied her eyes, but there was no sign of the hunger. Just irritation.

"Where did you get this?"

"I found it," I said.

She seized me by the collar and shoved me against the wall.

"Where?" she asked.

"Around."

She held me there. The universe didn't seem interested in intervening. Its protection was obviously not as great as advertised. She squinted, and her eyes turned a darker shade of blue. Whatever she saw, she didn't like. No surprise there. Most people didn't care for it.

"Did Monty give you this?"

"I know Monty."

It wasn't a direct answer to her question, but she let me go.

"Idiot," she said.

"Sorry."

"Not you." She appraised me. "Maybe you, but that's not important right now."

She went to my table and reached behind her back, producing a silver chalice from nowhere like Bugs Bunny pulling a mallet. The cup was like a souvenir found at a higher-end renaissance faire. The kind that has the extraneous *e* at the end of the word fair and way too many jugglers. She set it down on the table.

"I bear the cup."

"Ah, cool. It's . . . uh . . . nice."

"Are you a moron?"

"Depends on who you ask."

"Monty gave you his sword, then?"

"I found it."

She shook her head, and her long green hair moved slowly through the air like seaweed floating in the ocean. "A thing like this isn't just found, and this particular thing was never meant to be found again."

"I don't know what to tell you. I dug it up. Maybe you should talk to Monty."

"He wasn't meant to be found again either," she said. "Have you seen any signs of the dragon yet?" she asked.

"No. No dragons."

"Not dragons. Dragon. One. *THE* Dragon. Never mind."

She sat at the table, looked to my golf bag, to me, to her cup.

"I'm Ortiz," I said.

She considered the introduction a long while. I'd been involved in enough shady business to get it. She wondered if she should get her fingerprints on this mess.

"Gwen," she spit out through clenched teeth. "Why did you put the sword in that golf bag?"

"I thought it was better that way. Safer."

She looked inside. "Why the towel?"

"Extra safer?"

Her look let me know it was stupid, but the joke was on her. I already knew it was stupid.

"So you know how this works?" I asked. "This magic stuff."

"Nobody really knows how it works. Monty and the sword being back and you having it is proof enough of that."

"Okay, but you know more than me."

"I don't imagine that's too difficult."

The way she kept insulting me was distracting. I guess I had a type.

"Is there a way to turn it down? Like not shut it off, but keep it from screwing with people's heads?"

"Already? How long have you had it?"

I did some quick math. "Thirteen hours."

"Damn it. That's too fast."

"I don't know what to tell you then. Because there are currently two kids buried under a building. A couple of other guys, too, but those guys were assholes, so they don't bother me as much."

"All boons have a pull. Mortals desire them, and they desire to be used. But that's why we bearers exist. While we hold the boons that call is quieted. The world is safe from their influence unless we choose to lend them to a chosen mortal. And we stopped doing that for the good of everyone. But that sword is different. It can't be tamed. The sword . . . it's just bad news. It's why we got rid of it."

She moved toward me. I stepped back, afraid she'd smack me across the head, unsure if the sword would do anything about it, not sure if I wanted it to do anything about it if it meant destroying this building.

"Why would Monty give it to you?"

"He didn't. I told you. I found it."

"Monty bears that sword. Not you."

"He said something about both of us bearing it now."

"Not possible. There is only ever one bearer at a time. That's how it works."

"You said that nobody really knows how it works."

Her surprise was obvious. I'd won the debate.

She said, "Throw the sword out the window."

"That won't work," I replied.

"Humor me."

I pulled the sword out of the bag and chucked it out the window into the street below.

She folded her arms and smirked at me. "So where is it then?"

Some strange instinct compelled me to throw the rumpled blanket off my bed. The sword lay there on the sheets. It was a foregone conclusion, but it was a nice bit of showmanship on the sword's part. It was worth it just to see Gwen's face fall.

"Fucking hell."

She collected her thoughts.

"It's easy to think you've seen everything after you've been around long enough, but this is . . . this isn't right. We have to talk to Leo."

I dropped my sword back into the golf bag. "Who's Leo?"

"Leo is the guy who was supposed to be keeping an eye on all of this."

She waved her hands over her cup, and it vanished like a sleight of hand trick. She opened my closet door. The closet was gone. In its place, a hallway made of red bricks lit by flickering torches.

"How did you do that?" I asked.

"Doors work differently in the Dreaming World." She walked past the threshold and into the shadowy depths. Barely a silhouette, she glanced over her shoulder. "Are you coming?"

"Is it safe?"

"If you're a bearer," she said. "You're always safe."

"I thought you said I wasn't a bearer."

"I guess this is a way to find out for certain."

"What happens if I'm not?"

"It probably won't work for you."

"Probably?"

"Even people deep in the Waking World sometimes cross into the Dreaming one. It's where you get stories of the strange and inexplicable. Sometimes, someone absently opens a door and ends up somewhere they didn't expect. Sometimes, they don't even open a door."

I said, "Where does this door go?"

"I already told you. We're going to see Leo. Or I am. Whether you come along is up to you." She disappeared into darkness.

I considered the path before me. I could stay here in my apartment, play it safe. Or I could step through to some great unknown and seek out the answers to great, impossible truths.

Gwen's voice floated from the dark. "What are you doing?"

"I'm thinking," I said.

"Let me put this a different way," she said. "You have stepped into the Dreaming World. You can't hide from it. It will come for you, whether you like it or not. Now, would you rather be caught unprepared when it arrives or would you like to possibly be forewarned?"

"Can you just fix the sword for me?" I asked.

No answer came.

I'd never been brave. I blamed my upbringing, genetics, bad luck, my own lack of drive. Depended on the day, really. The bravest thing I'd ever done was steal money from Horace. That had been more stupid than brave and would've gotten me killed if not for supernatural intervention.

Gwen's disembodied voice said, "Are you really still thinking?"

She mumbled some insults, probably hoping to shame me into following her. But I'd learned to live shamefully.

"This is a lot," I said. "I need a minute."

Her voice softened. "Okay. That's fair."

"It is?"

"You're in the deep end," she said. "You have a right to be overwhelmed. It's hard for me to put myself in your place. It's been a long time, but this was easier for me. Things were more magical then. The barrier between the Waking and Dreaming Worlds blurrier. Take a moment to adjust. The world isn't going to end in the next five minutes, but you have to come with me."

I doubted she could force me because she probably would have already if that was possible. But if I was to get a handle on any of this I couldn't sit here and wait for the answers to come to me. So I screwed up what little courage I had and slung my golf bag over my shoulder.

"Fuck it. Let's go."

I stepped into the hall. My eyes adjusted to the dimness. It was just wide enough for Gwen and me to walk beside each other, but I didn't know her that well, so I trailed behind.

"Are we in the Dreaming World now?" I asked.

"Bearers are always in the Dreaming World," she said. "Imagine that your whole life you've been asleep, and you mistook that dream for reality. But now you're awake, and the longer you stay awake, the more you'll realize how limited your view of reality was."

"When I was asleep, I was in the Waking World. Now that I'm awake, I'm in the Dreaming World."

"It's called the Dreaming World because it's more flexible than the Waking one. In the Waking World, doors lead where you expect. In the Dreaming one, they lead to where you want them to lead. It's like lucid dreaming. You suddenly realize that things don't fit together the way they should, and for a moment, you understand that this isn't real. And then you wake up. Except now you can't wake up. That's why we call it the Dreaming World."

"Seems needlessly confusing," I said.

She sighed. "I didn't make up the damn names."

We reached a door at the end of the hall. She opened it, and we stepped into a barren landscape. Just black dirt and flat stones scattered about. The alien sky had no stars. There was something like a moon, but it was small and gray, casting a faint silver glow. A smell like damp laundry permeated the air.

A malformed creature, like a cross between a dog and a lizard but with too many legs and a head bent at the wrong angle, clawed its way across our path. Its every step was accompanied by a high-pitched gurgle, as if begging for death.

It did not surprise me that my personal Narnia was a shithole.

"This Leo guy lives here?" I asked.

"He volunteered."

She picked a direction and walked. I didn't see any landmarks to go by, but she seemed to know where she was going. When we moved too fast, we risked catching up to the horizon, like a video game struggling to render objects.

I said, "If doors lead to where you want, why did you make us walk this far?"

"This obscurity is remote. You can't just open a door and walk to it."

"Obscurity?"

"I'm not going to answer every stupid question you have. I'm not your tour guide. You'll figure it out on your own eventually. Just remember that there are rules even in the Dreaming World, but they're more metaphysical guidelines."

I decided to stop asking those stupid questions and take Gwen at her word. I'd gotten along fine without understanding the real world, if one used a broad enough definition of fine.

Eventually, we came across a building. The structure was made of the same flat stones that littered the ground. Thousands of them. Maybe millions. All stacked in a tower that went up higher than the physics of this place would allow me to see. It didn't go straight up, but had a slight corkscrew pattern to its rise. There were windows placed randomly in the structure and a single wooden door before us.

"Let me do the talking." She knocked. The whole building swayed ever so slightly with the disturbance.

The door immediately opened, and a man in a long red bathrobe stepped halfway out. He might have been black, but that could have been only an impression because his skin was dark brown wood. His hair was grass, and leaves poked out of his sleeves.

"I was wondering when you'd show up," he said.

"You were expecting me?" asked Gwen.

"Not you. Or him." He studied me for a long moment. "Definitely not him. But it was only a matter of time before someone showed up at my door bearing bad news."

"The sword is back."

"Impossible. I would've noticed."

She put her arm around me, pushing me forward. "Tell it to him."

She stepped across the threshold, leaving me face-to-face with Leo.

I felt myself being judged. I was used to it, but it didn't usually work out in my favor.

He asked, "Do you have a name?"

"Jay."

"Like the bird?"

"Like the bird. Most people call me Ortiz."

Leo straightened. His wooden body creaked slightly. It was only when he stood that I realized he'd been slouching. He was easily a foot taller than me.

He offered me his hand, which I took. The smooth wood was cool to the touch.

"Few souls have entered my home. Fewer still were worthy of the honor. Tell me, Ortiz"—he squeezed tighter—"are you worthy?"

Gwen shouted from inside. "Knock it off, Leo. He's having a hard enough time as it is, and we've got bigger problems."

The lines in the bark of his face crinkled as he smiled.

"I'm just screwing with you, Ortiz." He smacked me on the shoulder, and I nearly fell over. "There's no love lost between Gwen and me, so if she's bringing you here, then you must be a truly interesting fellow. Come in, then."

He moved with deliberate grace. Every step felt measured. Every gesture predetermined a thousand years before. I didn't so much follow him inside as creep after him apologetically.

The interior could only be described as rustic with tall shelves filled with books, and a fireplace with gently crackling orange flames. Gwen sat in a large leather chair by the fire, drinking a cup of tea.

"I don't know how you drink this crap. Got any honey around here?"

He waved her out of his way. She got up, then performed a long and low bow. Unamused, he sat. He folded his hands in his lap. His eyes glittered in the light of the fireplace.

"So what's this claptrap about the sword?" he asked.

She said, "That's what I like about you, Leo. You're the only guy I know who uses claptrap unironically. Go on, Ortiz. Show him."

I pulled the sword out of the bag.

"He wrapped it in a towel," said Gwen with a smirk. "For protection."

"Better safe than sorry," said Leo without a hint of sarcasm. "Care to unwrap it?"

I worked at the towel for a bit until Gwen handed me an old letter opener to tear away the duct tape.

"It certainly resembles Monty's sword," said Leo. "Did he give it to you, Ortiz?"

"He claims he found it," said Gwen.

"Then Monty's gone for good?" Leo topped off his cup of tea and took a delicate sip. "Then maybe we don't have a problem after all. The sword was only part of the problem."

"Monty is back, too. He says they're sharing it now."

"Why's that matter?" I asked.

They both looked at me like a dumb child.

Leo said, "Monty could lend you the sword. For a time. Or he could transfer it, making you its new bearer."

"Right," she said. "But what if there's a third thing Monty could've done?"

"Those are the only two possibilities."

"Come on. You feel it the same way I do. It feels like Monty is in the room, but also, like he's not in the room. It feels like that sword is halfway between where it belongs. It feels like—"

"Like a foundational stone of the universe has been shifted," said Leo. "And now everything has a slight wobble to it. Yes, I sense it."

He stared into the fire and tapped his finger against the back of his hand, producing small knocks barely audible in the room. "Does the dragon below still sleep?"

"Viv says it's been fitful. That's why she sent me to take a look. As soon as I stepped into the Waking World, I felt the sword." She pointed to me. "And this guy."

"Interesting."

They studied me quietly.

"Yes, interesting," Leo said, "but if the dragon below still sleeps, then perhaps we have nothing to worry about."

"That dragon isn't the problem," said Gwen.

"I thought you said there was only one dragon," I said.

"There are many," said Leo. "Dragons can represent many things. But we generally only worry about one Dragon, the embodiment of destruction."

"Sounds bad," I said.

"Assigning value to the Dragon is a human construct. It's like placing a moral judgment on gravity. It's good when it keeps you from floating off into space. It's bad when it's yanking you off a cliff. The Dragon is neutral, necessary even. But if it's returned, we should check on it."

"Yeah, good luck with that." Gwen headed toward the door.

Leo shook his head. "That's it, then? You drop this problem in my lap and then leave me to deal with it?"

"I need to tell Viv what's going on."

"You're reporting to her now?" he asked.

"No, but she should know."

"You're not fooling me. You just don't want to go near the Gorge."

"Would you?"

She exited, shutting the door behind her.

"Who's Viv?" I asked.

"Someone you don't need to concern yourself with. If you carry that sword long enough, you'll meet her. Tell her hello from me when you do."

Leo fixed me with a blank stare. His grandfatherly vibe remained, but now it was the vibe of a grandpa stuck with the grandkids when he'd much rather be out golfing.

"This must have been a surprising turn of events for you," he said.

I nodded. "I'm still wrapping my head around it."

He stood and put a hand on my shoulder. "If it makes you feel any better, I'm as surprised as you. And that means something, given I am ancient."

It did make me feel better.

"I should thank you, Ortiz. It's nice to have a mystery after all this time. Keeps the blood flowing. Without you, I might sit in that goddamn chair for a thousand years. Hell, maybe I already have."

He stretched, audibly creaking.

"Who's up for a field trip?"

CHAPTER FIVE

"We'll talk more on the way. We should get to it."

"Get to what?" I asked.

"The Dragon, of course. There might be answers there. No promises."

"Do you need me for that?"

"You? No. But we will need your sword, and it's yours to carry."

"So maybe I give it to you for a little while. Long enough for you to find the answers?"

Leo laughed. "Forgive me. I forgot that you don't know how any of this works. You can't transfer the sword to me. I already bear a boon."

He snapped his fingers and a tall, twisted branch grew out of his hand. It curled its way to the floor.

"I carry the staff."

"Maybe we find someone else, then? Just temporarily."

His face soured. His knothole eyes narrowed. "You have been chosen to carry a burden unworthy of lesser souls, and in less than a day you seek to throw that burden on another's shoulders?"

"I've never been great with responsibility."

"Consider this your chance to grow into it, then." He grunted. "The transference process is irreversible. Fatally so. The universe doesn't take kindly to those who challenge its wisdom."

"I'm stuck with this thing forever?"

"Until you decide you'd rather be dead than carry it." He leaned the staff across his shoulder. "How do you think I got this? And one day, when the weight of eternity becomes too much to bear, I'll do the same."

"Monty didn't seem dead," I said.

"Monty should be more than dead, but he's not. And we won't find answers here." He took one last sip of his tea and knocked his wooden hands together. "Let's get to it, then."

"Do you want to get changed?" I asked.

He was still wearing his bathrobe.

"I'm fine." He went to a hanging tapestry. It bore a crest of arms with a dragon and a unicorn. He gave it a hard yank, and it fell, kicking up a bunch of dust. I sputtered and sneezed. Wiping my watering eyes, I saw the door. "Was hoping to never have to use this again."

The knob jiggled in his hand. "Stubborn today. I know I have the key somewhere around here, but you have the sword. If you'd be so kind."

I approached the door. The golf bag slung over my shoulder felt heavy against my back, like it was pushing me forward. When I was within a few steps, the door popped open on its own.

"The sword seeks its home." Leo opened the door the rest of the way slowly, as if the slightest creak in its hinges would cause the universe to explode. Beyond the threshold was nothing but black.

"It's not as scary as it looks." He stepped through, swallowed by the emptiness.

I followed. This time there was no hesitation. The pull was just too strong.

On the other side, the first thing I noticed was the absolute stillness of the air and the crushing silence.

We were surrounded by junk. There was a pile of shields of all shapes and sizes and materials twice as tall as Leo. Beside that, stacks of precariously balanced books. Mountains of swords and axes and helmets and cloaks stretched to the horizon.

"Welcome to the Gorge's edge."

He led me among the junk. There was no end as far as I could see. A sky full of unbroken gray clouds swirled overhead. A soft light filtered through them. Silent lightning flashed in the clouds, and a few objects fell from the sky. Each piece of debris seemed presorted, landing into mountains of the same type.

"Where are we?" I asked.

"An obscurity. A little bubble of its own reality floating at the edges of the Dreaming World. It's unclear what these are. I think most are remnants, pieces of the worlds that never were or could have been or never should be. Cast-off bits that became woven into the fabric of the universe, but ended up buried and concealed, just out of sight. Tell me, Ortiz, have you ever had the feeling, however fleeting, that behind that next corner is a world waiting for you to discover it?"

"No, not really."

He stopped suddenly and pursed his lips. "How sad for you. Though I think it was more common in the older times, when the world was fresh and unmapped. Before humanity explored it, erasing so many of its mysteries."

He started walking again. "But some of those mysteries refused to go quietly. They remain, waiting to be found, growing sullen and hostile in their loneliness."

"We're not in any danger here, are we?"

"I carry this staff. The universe will see no harm comes to me. As for you . . . I don't know, but you made it this far. You're probably fine."

In this endless plain of junk, there was a lot of wiggle room in that maybe, but I'd long ago figured that I'd die some stupid, pointless death, and that would've been true if not for the sword. I trusted it would keep me alive.

"Why is all this stuff here?"

"Don't tell me they've lost all the stories of the Dragon. It collects things. The discarded refuse, the forgotten things. These are its treasures."

I reached out toward a collection of vintage G.I. Joe and Barbie dolls, all in their original boxes but also faded and covered in dust.

Leo smacked my hand. There must have been a thorn on one of his fingers, because he drew blood.

"Mustn't touch. The Dragon guards its treasures."

I rubbed the wound. So much for safe.

We carried on in silence. If felt like an hour passed. It might have been longer or shorter. There was no way to tell since there didn't appear to be day or night here.

"Tell me, Ortiz, do you know of the Sword of Damocles?" asked Leo out of the blue. He continued without waiting. Probably because he'd figured out the answer.

"I'll give you the short version. There's a king and a peasant. The peasant says it must be great to be king, so the king makes him an offer. The peasant can be king for as long as he's willing to sit on the throne. The catch is that a sword is hung, point down, over the throne by a frayed thread that threatens to break at any moment."

"Sounds like a bad deal," I said.

"Personally, I think it's a bullshit story kings tell peasants to convince them to be happy with their lot in life. We all walk around with tragedy hanging over our heads. Only kings get a story telling everyone it's something special about them."

"Is that my sword?" I asked.

"Yes and no. A sword, like a story, can represent many things."

"Why are you telling me this?"

"Just something to think about," said Leo with a wink. "We're almost there."

A little farther or maybe a thousand miles—the whole place was screwing with my head—the mountains of junk parted, and the uneven ground sloped sharply upward. A massive hole in the ground stood before us in the rocky outcropping. Despite the angle, it was as if one step too close would cause me to plummet into it. Black and green stones ringed it in a jagged irregular pattern. We snaked around them like weaving through the teeth of a giant mouth, and came to the edge. As close as we dared. A little closer than I would've wanted, honestly.

The Gorge was inky darkness. It devoured the light like a black hole. It pulled me toward it. Leo put a hand on my shoulder.

"Mind that last step."

I was a lot closer to the edge than I realized.

"It's hungry," he said. "Always hungry."

"The Gorge or the Dragon?"

"They are one and the same. Left unchecked, it would consume everything."

"That's what the sword is for," I said.

Leo smiled. "You sense it, don't you?"

I felt something. A cosmic string connecting me to the sword and the sword to the Dragon. Vibrating with anticipation.

"The Dragon serves a purpose, but it is ultimately driven by a singular need. Its endless hunger can never be sated. If it were let loose without restraint it would devour the universe. And in the dark emptiness, it would dwell forever alone and still unsatisfied."

I took the sword from the bag. "I shouldn't have this. I'm a fuckup."

"Perhaps you judge yourself too harshly."

"Oh no. This isn't low self-esteem talking. This is just a goddamn fact."

I let go of the sword. It clattered at my feet.

The world quaked. A hot wind exploded from the Gorge. It stank of rot and pestilence.

"Well, isn't that interesting?" said Leo.

"Is it awake?" I grabbed Leo by the robe. "Did I just wake this fucking thing?"

He gently pushed me away. "You tell me."

I heard something stirring in the Gorge's bottomless depths. Something vast. Something starving. Its breaths slow and steady, a behemoth at the edge of sleep.

I stood over the sword, afraid to touch it. "We shouldn't be here. Why did you bring me here?"

"Because it's important you know what you're dealing with. Because if my suspicions are true then you'll have to be ready sooner than you think."

"Ready for what?"

He leaned on his staff with an enigmatic grin.

"Let me tell you a story, Ortiz."

"Another Sword of Damocles metaphor?"

"No metaphors. Just a bit of history."

He leaned his weight against his staff, suddenly seeming very tired.

"None can say where the boons came from, but there's no doubt of their influence over humanity. Each boon seeks out a bearer, who bestows it upon the worthy. And those judged worthy shape the history of the world in ways both visible and invisible."

I said, "I know it's been a while since you've been to the world, but it's not great out there."

"No, I'm sure it isn't. And it never has been. The system is flawed down to the core. Humanity is fallible, foolish, shortsighted, greedy, temperamental . . . well, I don't suppose I have to tell you all that. We bearers, whether chosen by fate or simply happenstance, are still human. But, worst of all, the boons themselves are beyond anyone's understanding.

"Each has a grand purpose that it seeks to fulfill once in human hands. This staff I carry creates wisdom and guidance. Gwen's cup embodies compassion and healing. And that sword you hold is aggression and ambition—but also, it's tasked with holding off the Dragon.

"Bearers spent ages bestowing our boons. Grand deeds were performed, but also, smaller miracles forgotten to legend. All steps to help humanity crawl from the muck of fear and ignorance. Mistakes happened, but despite that, progress was made. There was some debate among the bearers whether the boons had the greater influence over the world or they were merely an expression of the Dreaming World's desires, but it was all academic.

"The bearers carried their burdens, and when they found that burden overwhelming, they transferred that burden to another. This was necessary from time to time because a bearer is not beyond the influence of their boon. Over time, the bearer and the boon become closer, possibly indistinguishable."

"Is that why you're made of wood?" I asked.

"Physical transformation is a symptom, yes, but there are other, deeper effects. As the staff bearer, I'm compelled to act as a guide. Why do you think I'm telling you this, Ortiz?"

"Okay, so tell me what to do then."

"I offer guidance, not knowledge."

"There's a difference?"

"Yes, there is. I can't just spell it out for you. Then it wouldn't be wisdom."

"So you don't know how to fix this."

"I'm not an instruction manual on how to keep the world running properly. I'm more of a mirror reflecting the answers you will find within yourself."

"I don't have any answers."

"In that case, we're screwed, but I can only lay my guidance at your feet. It's not up to me if you have the tools to pick it up. But we're getting ahead of ourselves.

"Of all the boons, though, the most fearsome and terrible was that sword you've found yourself with. It is ambition manifest. Without that sword, humanity might never have dared rise out of its lowly origins. We might never have been anything more than primates happily playing in the trees."

"That doesn't sound so bad," I said.

"True enough, but can't stuff the genie back in the bottle. The sword exists, and with it, humanity saw the world as an adversary that could be beaten, and the world responded by unleashing the Dragon. So it became that the sword and the Dragon, opposing forces, struggled in a hateful equilibrium."

"You're saying the universe hates us?"

"A poor choice of words," Leo said. "It's more like it feels challenged by us, and like any threatened beast, its instinct is to lash out. The Dragon is that, but so long as the sword exists the balance is maintained."

"So what went wrong, then?"

"Monty went wrong. Bearers become their boons, and after bearing the sword for so long, it corrupted him. He became ambitious to a fault, and yet, he was never able to use its full power. That is the price of being a bearer. Most of us can live with that, and if we can't, we can always transfer it. But the nature of the sword meant that Monty could do neither. Eventually, it threatened to consume him, and in his madness, he hoped to break the rules.

"He couldn't, but he kept trying. Each attempt angering the Dragon and threatening to unravel everything. Obscurities started decaying and disappearing. There were wonders you may have heard of in legend that once existed somewhere. Now they're gone. Many are completely forgotten, even among bearers."

He closed his eyes.

"If I concentrate hard enough, I can almost see them like a dream half-remembered. There was a forest or a meadow, I think. Maybe a savanna. So beautiful that even with a shadow of it in my memory, even if I can't be sure it ever existed, I ache to see it."

He opened his eyes, and the pain was obvious enough for me to notice.

"No matter. What's gone is gone. The sword's corruption had affected the Waking World more subtly, but there were signs. Wars and death and the like. It wasn't that the sword made humanity more violent, but it did fill the human race with an endless thirst for conquest. Enough to tip things in dangerous directions."

"We're assholes because of this sword?"

"A simplification, but that sword certainly didn't help. Viv believed that it would only get worse. She tried convincing Monty to let go of the sword, but he couldn't. With no other choice, she and the other bearers lured him here and threw him and the sword into the Gorge, the one place there is no escape."

He looked at me, then at the Gorge.

"Hey, man, I'm cool," I said. "Not ambitious at all."

"If I was going to push you in, I wouldn't warn you in advance," said Leo.

Just the same, I stepped away from the edge, which I had unconsciously shifted near again.

"But without the sword what keeps the Dragon at bay?"

"The sword is both poison and antidote," said Leo. "As long as it exists, the Dragon is kept at bay, but it also challenges it. With the sword gone, it returned to the emptiness from which it came. It's always there. Gnawing at the roots of the world in its slumber, but more manageable.

"We hoped that by sacrificing the sword that it would be the end of it. Nothing escapes the Gorge. Or so we thought. But here you stand, with that fucking sword. And I fear that we only made things worse in our actions."

A searing wind erupted from the Gorge. Despite physics, I fell closer to the hole. Its invisible claws seized me by the ankle and yanked me closer still. In my panic I grabbed for anything to save me. My hand fell across something hot, and the force released me.

I scrambled a safe distance away. Safer. There was no safety. Not here. Maybe not anywhere. I clutched the sword in my hand. It was drawn to the Gorge, but it had pulled me away. Poison and antidote.

Monty stepped from the Gorge. "On the contrary, Leo, you showed me the way."

"Hello, Monty." Something danced under Leo's voice. Disgust. Pity. Regret. All of that and more.

Monty smiled. "Is that any way to greet an old friend?"

Leo said, "The Monty I knew died a long time ago. Long before we threw you in that hole. Now whatever has clawed its way out... I don't know who that is."

"Ouch. The way you talk, you'd think I was the one who conspired to betray you."

Monty stared into the Gorge.

"We've all been playing this game for a long time, and nothing has come of it. Why don't you tell him, Leo, about how the ages pass and you've all hidden away, too afraid to bestow your boons on the world. Always carrying power, but never being able to use it yourselves, yet never able to find anyone worthy of it either. Watching as the human race fumbles around like idiots, adrift. Tell him about the last time you bestowed that staff to someone. Or do you even remember?"

"You know I do."

"Of course you do. You'll never forget it, will you?"

"They're not ready," said Leo. "Not yet."

Monty shook his head. "They'll never be ready."

"If you felt that way, you could've transferred the sword and found peace."

Monty whirled. His body flared brighter. It should have been blinding, but magic was weird.

"Waiting around forever for the human race to be worthy doesn't do anybody any good. It's time to put up or shut up. It's time for the world to be reborn in a glorious age of enlightenment or be burnt to ash. Frankly, I don't really give a damn which way it goes."

"That's the sword talking," said Leo.

"I don't need that goddamn sword," said Monty. "Not anymore. Thanks to the Gorge. And to you."

He turned his head toward me as if noticing me for the first time. These two were elemental forces. And nobody smart wanted to be noticed by elemental forces.

"So you're playing god?" asked Leo.

"Gods are pathetic reflections of human fears and dreams."

Monty sprang upon Leo. He placed a hand upon Leo's shoulder, and I could smell the stench of burning wood. Leo screamed as he dropped to one knee.

The ground quaked. The piles of junk on the horizon fell over. The Dragon stirred within the Gorge's depths. Its roar shattered the sky. The pieces came raining down like giant glass prisms. They broke all around us, disintegrating upon impact.

Monty, burning like a miniature sun, released Leo.

"And I'm through playing."

The Dragon's head emerged from the Gorge. Its skin was a kaleidoscope of shifting colors, ten thousand diamond scales generating their own light. Its jaws were a hungry chasm. The Gorge and the Dragon. One and the same.

It dragged its immense bulk halfway out the Gorge, studying us with its burning red eyes. Looking at it, I realized I was only comprehending the barest portion of it. It was immeasurable. This was just me seeing a tooth or an eye and making it something I could grasp.

The same way it was beyond us, we were beneath it. We were things it couldn't understand. It was a primordial force wearing an unconvincing skin. It was the fire blazing through an ancient forest without malice or hate, only hunger. It was the goddamn atomic bomb on great golden wings.

Its gaze fixed on me, and I realized I had the sword in my hands. I didn't remember picking it up.

"You can't use it," said Monty.

"What am I supposed to do, then?"

He wasn't the guy to ask, but I was desperate. He only laughed.

The Dragon roared. With one beat of its wings, it flew into the broken sky.

Leo, his shoulder still smoldering, stood. "What have you done?"

But Monty was gone, and the Dragon along with him.

CHAPTER SIX

Monty's handprint was seared into Leo's wooden shoulder. "I thought you couldn't be hurt."

"A day full of surprises, some unpleasant," said Leo. "I'd forgotten what pain was like."

"Is there something I can do? Maybe get you to a doctor?"

"It's nothing." He steadied himself. "We have more important things to worry about."

Up to this moment, Leo had seemed eternal, invulnerable, but now he was just some guy. Monty's handprint had burned away the bark, exposing the blistered, blackened skin beneath. He was flesh and blood under there.

The ground shook as part of it fell away into the Gorge. The Dragon may have flown away, but the Gorge still hungered.

"What's going to happen now?" I asked.

He shrugged, wincing at the pain in his shoulder.

"The Dragon is loosed. Disaster is sure to follow until it is tamed again. But I wouldn't say it's the end of the world. Then again, my centuries of experience don't seem to count for much lately. Still, once you find the right person to bestow the sword upon, things should get back in order, despite whatever Monty has done."

"Who is the right person?"

"That's the question, isn't it?"

He hobbled away, using his staff as a walking stick. "We should go before we end up in the Gorge."

I was closer to the edge than I'd realized. Again. I suspected the Gorge moved when we weren't paying attention, creeping toward its prey. It couldn't swallow you all on its own, but all it would take was one misstep and then a long fall into nothingness.

"Just walk," said Leo. "Don't look back. Ignore the Gorge, like you have the inevitable oblivion that pursues every mortal life."

We walked. It might have been that I was adjusting to these weird rules, but time fell away and it didn't bother me. Here, in these between places, I didn't have to worry about anything. And then I found a pile of old doors.

"Hang on," I said. "I think I can get us out of here."

I tried opening a door. It didn't work.

"Nice try," said Leo. "You're learning."

He struggled to pull a door off the pile. I helped him drop it flat on the ground. He lifted it by the handle, revealing a staircase made of gray stone leading into the earth. I carried him down. Ten feet down, we came across another door that I opened.

It led to that lonely little room again with the rune-inscribed chair.

"You should sit," I said.

"No." Leo pulled away from me, almost falling over. "Don't sit in that chair."

"Okay."

"Listen to me, Ortiz. Don't ever sit in that chair."

"Evil chair. Understood."

"It's not evil," he said. "Just don't sit in it."

"I'm not arguing," I replied.

Leo staggered closer, grabbing me by the collar. "Just don't sit in it. No matter what it promises."

The chair itself stood there, not doing much of anything, which, given the situation, did make it a little suspect. Using dream logic, a chair this ordinary looking had to have something wrong with it. And dream logic had gotten me this far, to a room under the earth with dangerous—but not evil—furniture.

"Where do we go from here?" I asked.

Leo closed and opened the door we came in, the only exit. My apartment was now on the other side. I helped him across the threshold, shutting the door behind us.

"This is where you live?" asked Leo.

"It's not much, but it's home." I cleared some dirty clothes off the couch for him, and he sat, trying and failing to stifle a groan as he did.

"Are you sure you're okay?" I asked.

"I'll need a few minutes."

He closed his eyes. I couldn't tell if he was breathing or photosynthesizing.

"Just a few..." he mumbled.

I found an old pan, filled it with water, and sat it down by the couch, gently placing his right foot in it. No idea if it would help, but worth a shot.

The front door opened. In a panic, I thought about grabbing some of that dirty laundry and throwing it onto Leo, but it was a stupid idea.

Irene entered. "Why haven't you been answering your phone?"

"I've been... out."

I checked my phone. There were a few calls and texts from Irene.

"You need to get out of town," she said. "Horace called in Raul."

"It's okay," I said.

She walked past me to sit on the couch beside Leo without acknowledging him or the pan of water. I wondered how the Waking and Dreaming Worlds overlapped, but it made things easier, so I just went with it.

She said, "It's not okay, you dumbass. Raul is a fucking psycho."

I'd never worked directly with Raul. He didn't like me, and I was grateful for that because I had cleaned up after Raul two times, and in a business full of people that hurt people professionally, Raul loved his work in a way few did.

"You need to go before he finds you," she said. "And since you're in your own goddamn apartment, I'm betting he finds you pretty soon."

"It's not a problem," I said.

"How is it not a problem?"

I pulled the sword out of the golf bag. "Because I have this."

Irene sat across from me at the kitchen table, giving me that look of hers.

"I know how it sounds," I said.

"Do you?" She tapped her lighter on the table as she chewed on a cigarette.

I put my hand on hers. "I wouldn't believe it either, but I've seen things since yesterday that I can't explain otherwise."

"So magic exists, and you have a magic sword. Like King Arthur."

"I think it's more like I'm Merlin," I replied. "I'm just holding the sword."

"Merlin wasn't in charge of the sword," she said.

"Let's not get bogged down in the specifics."

She stood, struck up the lighter, but didn't light the cigarette. She almost said something before turning her back, mumbling to herself. I thought about saying something, but there wasn't any way to soften this. It just had to play out. Anything I did say was more likely to sound stupider than it already sounded.

She turned back, gestured impatiently. "Can I touch it?"

"That might not be a good idea," I said. "It might affect you."

"How?"

"It can fuck with people's minds."

"I'm going to lose my mind if I touch it for a few seconds?"

I looked to Leo for guidance. He sat unmoving on my couch. The faint stink of decay hit me, a combination of moldy fern and infected flesh. Either Irene hadn't noticed, or she chalked it up to my poor housekeeping.

She leaned forward, hands on table. "Ortiz, sweetie, I am going to need more than a discount store sword to buy any of this."

It wasn't an unreasonable request.

"I'm not responsible for what happens." I held it out, blade toward her.

"Since when have you ever been responsible?"

She reached out, but I pulled it away.

"Just a touch," I said.

She put her fingers on the flat of the blade. I waited for any signs of madness as she stepped away. She paced back and forth, looking to me, then the sword, then me. Sighing, she stuck the cigarette back in her pocket and sat at the table.

"All right. I believe you."

"You do?"

She glared. "You want me to believe you, don't you?"

"Yes, but . . . well . . . it's a lot."

"Not really," she said. "It explains some things. Like how you're still alive after stealing from Horace."

"I could be smart," I said.

She smiled. "Oh, honey . . ."

"I could be lucky."

Her sly grin turned into a chuckle. "Oh, come on. We both know your luck."

"Maybe that just means I'm due for a win."

"Guys like you don't win, Ortiz."

"Then why are you with me?" I asked.

She shrugged. "You were the best guy of a lousy selection."

"You should write Hallmark cards," I said.

She said, "I've narrowed it down to three possibilities. Either you're smart. Or you're lucky. Or you've got a magic sword that's kept you alive. Fuck me, but we both know the sword is the most believable explanation."

"Interesting," said Leo.

She jumped. I jumped, too, because I'd placed odds that he was dead.

"Is that a talking tree?" she asked.

"That's Leo," I said. "You can see him now?"

"Now? How long has he been sitting there? And is he made of wood?"

"It's complicated," I replied.

Leo struggled to stand.

"Maybe you should stay down," I said.

"There's no time." He leaned against his staff. "Funny. I thought myself immortal until I chose otherwise. I thought I'd have plenty of time, but the promises of the universe are so much bullshit in the end."

He paused, sucking in a painful breath.

"Why am I standing in water?"

He stepped out of the pan.

"It is a grave responsibility I must now pass onto you. If I had more time I would find a more suitable candidate, but I'm almost gone. You must take the staff. It's yours to bear."

"I already have the sword," I said, "and I shouldn't even have that."

"Not you."

He limped toward Irene. "You're not my first choice, but circumstances are what they are. So take it."

I stepped between them. "No, don't take it. You can't make her take it."

"Make her?" He laughed, a dry wheeze that racked his fragile body. Pieces of bark flaked off, and his leaves grayed as they fell away. "It's an honor. One she is unworthy of, but beggars can't be choosers."

He tried to push me aside, but he was much too weak.

"If I die while bearing the staff," he said, "then the staff dies with me."

I kept myself firmly planted between them. "She doesn't want it."

"Maybe I do," she said.

"No, you don't."

"Why do you get to decide for me?" she asked. "You can't even manage your own life."

"Can we not fight about this?"

"That's not an answer," she said.

"It's her decision," whispered Leo.

She tried to step around me, but I outmaneuvered her.

"Just please do what I ask this once," I said.

It was the wrong thing to say. Irene didn't like being told what to do. She especially didn't like being told what to do by fuckups. And looking back on it, maybe there was also the draw of the staff itself. It didn't want to die.

"Ortiz, I swear to god if you don't get out of my way . . ."

I wondered if the sword would protect me from her, the same way it had protected me in the past. How would it react if she did something stupid? How would it interpret any hostility?

The universe might simply slap her on the wrist or it could explode my kitchen stove, sending a piece of shrapnel through her brain. Just the first possibility that ran through my mind. There were infinitely more I couldn't think of.

I stepped aside.

Leo smiled through his pain as he handed her the staff. "May you bear its burden better than any before you."

A spark passed between them. Strands of light appeared on the staff, connected to Leo. They dissolved one by one as new ones attached themselves to Irene. The last strand clung as if it didn't want to let go, but when Leo released the staff, the connection shattered.

He fell back onto the couch, slumping to one side.

The lights faded, and Irene pulled the staff closer, holding it in two hands. "That was neat. Was that what it was like for you?"

"You should've listened to me and not taken it."

"So you're the guy who gets a magic sword, and I get nothing?"

She spun the staff in small circles. "I don't know. This feels right to me. Like it was always meant to be mine. What powers do I get?"

She held up the staff and deepened her voice.

"Let my people go."

Nothing happened.

"We don't get powers. Not like that. You're supposed to become an embodiment of guidance and wisdom. Eventually."

"Really?" She sneered at the boon. "What a rip-off. I was hoping for three wishes. What's the sword supposed to be?"

"Ambition. Aggression."

"Then how the hell did you end up with it?"

"I don't know."

She nodded at Leo's body on my couch. "Is he dead?"

"You're supposed to be wise. You tell me."

He raised his head. "No. Not dead. Not quite yet, but getting there. One last task left to me. A lingering duty." He struggled to straighten himself. He lifted a trembling hand toward me. "With the Dragon returned, you must find the strength to give it to someone to use."

"To who?" I asked.

"Whom," he said. "And that's your choice to make."

"Come on," I said. "Just tell me. You're dying. Why do you still have to follow these stupid rules?"

He smiled politely, as if explaining how to play *Candy Land* to a toddler. "To get the most out of the sword, you must find the right user. In the right hands, the Dragon can be driven back. It might not solve the problem, but it will give us time." He leaned forward, almost falling over until Irene and I caught him. "The sword will tempt you, which is why you must give it away as quickly as possible. As a bearer, you can't use it, but the longer you hold it, the more likely you will fall victim to it. Like Monty did."

"I don't want it," I said. "I shouldn't have it."

Leo said, "No one should, but you'd be surprised how few realize that." He put a hand to my face, looked me deep in the eyes. "There is hope for us yet, I think."

"Hope for who?" I asked.

With a slight smile, he burst into flame, burning from the inside out in a bright blue green. In a few seconds he was nothing but a pile of charcoal on my blackened couch and carpet, leaving behind the stench of a squirrel roasted in a forest fire.

Irene asked, "Who is Monty?"

I held the sword. "Monty's my problem."

"Looks like he might have been his problem, too. And now that I have this staff, I'm assuming he's my problem as well."

I swept up Leo's remains and dropped them in the garbage. I thought about saying something in his memory, but I didn't know the guy.

I hefted the golf bag over my shoulder. "I guess we should find someone to use the sword."

"Who?"

"Whom," I replied. "And I've got no clue."

CHAPTER SEVEN

Before giving the sword to someone, Irene had me drive down to the corner store where she bought some gum and a handful of scratch-off tickets. Chewing on her gum, she scratched all the tickets. They weren't all winners, but in the end, twenty bucks in tickets netted us a return of twenty bucks. She took the tickets back in to buy more and got the same results. The third time yielded predictable results.

"Breaking even isn't much of a super power," she said.

"Maybe the universe doesn't want us to be rich," I said.

"Yeah, well the universe can kiss my ass." Irene blew a big bubble, letting it grow to dangerous proportions before it finally popped. Against the odds, none of it stuck to her face, which I took as supernatural intervention. "So what happens after you give the sword to someone?"

"They'll send the Dragon packing, and then, we'll be free and clear. We pack our bags. We take our money, and we get out of this town."

"That's it?" she asked. "What about Horace?"

"He can't hurt us now."

"And that's enough for you? After the way he treated you, you're just going to let him get away with it?"

"Horace did all right by me," I said.

"He tried to have you killed. Twice."

"Nobody made me hitch my wagon to his star," I said. "Horace never pretended to be anybody other than he was. I stole his money. I knew the deal if he caught me."

"Sounds like you're on his side." She got out of the car, slamming the door as she went back into the store to cash in her scratch-offs.

I'd messed up somehow. Irene and I had our thing. I thought I wanted it to be more than that, but our relationship was a beat-up jalopy on a rough road. It hadn't broken down yet, but every mile only increased the odds.

Maybe the universe would help with that now that we were bearers. We weren't regular people now. We were special. Then again, that might have made things harder. From what I'd seen of the other bearers they didn't like each other. That just might be the way this worked.

She returned to the car. She sat there, breaking even on scratch-offs while chewing her gum loudly. When I finally tried to say something, she stopped me.

"You're sorry. I know. You're always sorry." She pulled down the sun-visor mirror and applied some lip gloss. "But doesn't it piss you off? Guys like Horace go through life hurting everybody they come across and getting ahead. Meanwhile, guys like you just scrape by. Just sucks is all I'm saying."

"It's complicated," I replied. "Horace is a bad guy, but it's not an accident I work for him. I might be a petty criminal, but I've still done my share of bad stuff."

"You've never killed anyone." She realized then that she didn't technically know that. "You've never killed anyone, right?"

"No," I said. "Never killed anyone. Never broke anybody's knees. I punched a kid when I was twelve."

"See? You're not a bad guy."

"I've been in the room when people have been punched. I've been in the room when people were shot. Worse stuff."

"Like what?"

"Rather not talk about it, but I've helped bury too many bodies."

"Oh, baby." She leaned over and hugged me. "You just did what you had to do."

I'd already told myself that dozens of times. I could only do my best to survive. I gripped the steering wheel, staring straight ahead. "He never asked me to kill anyone. Never trusted me to not screw it up."

"You'd have said no," she said.

"I never told Horace no. And even before that I've never made the right decision, the good decision."

"You've never had a choice. But now, you do." She cradled the staff in her seat, across her shoulder. "We do."

She gripped it tight.

"Do you want to know why I never walked away from Horace?" she said.

"I just assumed you liked the money," I replied. "And the heated pool."

"How shallow do you think I am?"

"I've seen people do worse things for less," I said.

"If I cared about money I could've left any time. Horace would've taken care of me and been thankful to get rid of me. At least once a week he'd scream at me to get the fuck out of his house, and he'd get this look in his eyes. Like he wished he could just kill me, but mom's memory always kept him from doing it. Sometimes, I wasn't sure it would. But I still pushed that fucker." She laughed, stamping the staff in the floorboard. "Just poking and poking and poking him every day. I was the one thing he couldn't control, couldn't boss around, couldn't put a bullet in, and I made it my job to make that son of a bitch miserable because I was the only one who could."

I'd always assumed Horace and Irene's fights were due to Horace being Horace. Now I saw in her wicked smile that Irene had been doing her part. I sure knew how to pick them.

"And now I have this thing," Irene said, "this magical boon, and you're telling me that I can't do anything about him."

"I don't want to kill anyone. Not even Horace."

She looked shocked.

"I didn't say we should kill him. Why would you—" She sucked in a deep breath. "It just feels like we should be able to do something about him."

"Getting rid of a guy like Horace doesn't make the world a better place. It just grows another Horace in the vacuum. We have our boons. We have our money. Once we find the right person to bestow the sword upon, we can drive away without looking back."

"And that's enough for you?"

"We're not chosen ones. We aren't going to fix the world."

"They why do we have these? What's the point?"

"Maybe there's no point."

"Well, that's depressing."

I took her hand. "We still have each other."

"You're such a schmuck, Ortiz." But she leaned in and kissed me. "So who are you going to give it to?"

I pointed to a man walking out of the convenience store. "He looks fine."

I was halfway out the door when she grabbed my arm. "No, not him."

"Why not?"

"I don't like his vibe."

"Well, if it's a vibe thing . . ."

"I'm serious. I've had an epiphany."

"I don't think people like us have epiphanies," I replied, as I sat back down in my seat.

"These boons will make the person who carries them into important people, right? Like King Arthur and Excalibur or Jason and the Golden Fleece."

"Prince Adam and the Power Sword," I said.

"If that example works best for you," Irene said with a condescending smile. "So imagine if Skeleton Man got hold of the Power Sword."

"Skeletor," I said.

"Imagine if Skeletor got the Power Sword, what would happen?"

"He'd get into Castle Grayskull, and then, conquer the universe."

"Right. So what we don't need to do is make a Skeletor here."

"I don't think our boons are on that level. I guess we could maybe make an Evil-Lyn."

"It's like I'm dating a twelve-year-old," she said. "So we're not making the next king of Castle Grayskull, but if we give it to the wrong person, we could be doing a lot of damage."

"Grayskull doesn't have a king," I said.

She smacked me on the back of the head. "Why would the universe give you that sword?"

She wasn't wrong. I probably wouldn't make the next Hitler with my choice, but I'd feel like a real asshole if I did.

"Goddamn it," I grumbled.

Irene put her arm around me. "Epiphanies are a real bitch, huh?"

"How do we decide, then?" I asked.

"We need to make sure we give it to a good person."

"Where do we find a good person?" I said. "And we need to do it sooner than later because the sword will call to some people, making them crazy."

A woman pulled up on her motorcycle. She removed her helmet and made extended eye contact with me. Her expression was blank, but maybe I saw something covetous cross her face. Could have been my imagination.

Then a cop car pulled in for gas. "How about them?"

"Fuck the police," said Irene, as if she hailed from Compton instead of a cushy manor atop a hill overlooking the town. "But you're onto something. What about a fireman or an EMT? They're good people."

"So we start a fire?" I said.

"Whatever works," she said.

A siren blared as a fire truck drove down the street.

I said, "I told you the universe is watching out for us."

We followed the truck to a small building fire. It was nothing serious, but the truck and the lights and the outfits did have a certain romantic appeal. The firefighters had taken off their hats and unzipped the tops of their jumpsuits, standing in a circle.

One stepped forward as we approached. He couldn't have been a more perfect example of the job. Tall, broad shoulders, lantern jaw, smokey, piercing eyes, a smile that inspired confidence. If this man found you in a raging inferno, you wouldn't just survive. You'd go back to college, mend broken friendships, volunteer at soup kitchens. You'd spend the rest of your life proving yourself worthy of the intervention of this handsome, selfless angel of a human being. You'd fail, but you'd do your best.

"Sorry, folks, but you'll need to keep your distance." His deep voice rumbled out of his barrel chest and gave your ears a reassuring hug.

"Excuse me," said Irene. "I think you people are heroes."

"Just doing our job, ma'am. But thanks."

"Oh, modest. Modesty is the sign of a good person, right?" She prodded me with her elbow. "Give him the thing."

I pulled the sword from my golf bag and awkwardly offered it to him. I thought I should kneel. Or he should. One of us.

He took it without questioning its oddness as a gift. The power of a boon, I supposed. He smiled as he inspected it. "Thank you, sir."

"You're welcome," I said.

The chosen firefighter rejoined his fellows, who all congratulated him. No envy there, because this guy was the right guy. In his hands, the sword would find its ultimate potential, and the world would be better for it.

He climbed into his truck.

"You take care now," he said, "and check the batteries in your smoke detectors."

"Yes, sir." I saluted, and he chuckled.

"This is a good choice," said Irene as the truck drove away. "No, this was a great fucking choice."

The truck turned the corner, and all felt right for a moment. The universe had made its choice, and we had made ours. And now we could finally relax.

The sky darkened as something massive spread its wings overhead. A shadow threatened to swallow the city.

"What is that?" asked Irene.

"The Dragon."

The creature passed over us, flying in the direction of the fire truck. Nobody else on the street noticed. They were all in the Waking World.

"He has the sword. He should be fine, right?" she said.

I pushed away a buzz in my head. "Yeah. I'm sure he can handle it."

The ground quaked, and the block's lights flickered. The Dragon towered over us. It was just large enough to clutch a fire truck in its jaws. It glared down at me with its hateful eyes as it snapped the truck in half with one bite.

The chosen firefighter, my chosen firefighter, crawled from the cab's wreckage. He had the sword in hand, but before he could stand, the Dragon snatched him up in its maw. He reached out to us a moment before the creature chewed and swallowed. His arm and a boot with or without a foot fell to the ground before us. My sword drove itself blade-first into the concrete.

The Dragon bellowed a pillar of cosmic fire into the darkness. It flapped its shining wings as it disappeared into the sky, letting the light back into the world.

CHAPTER EIGHT

We sat in my car, watching as they brought a couple of wreckers to collect the bisected fire truck.

"What the fuck was that?" asked Irene. "I thought giving him the sword was going to fix things."

"I guess it didn't."

"You killed those guys," she said.

"Me? You were the one who said I should give him the sword!"

"How was I supposed to know you'd listen to me for once?"

The sword in the golf bag sat in the back seat. I hadn't picked it up. It had followed me.

"What do we do now?" she asked.

"How would I know?"

I braced myself for whatever insult she was about to toss my way, but her eyes went wide as she looked past me.

"Ah, shit."

Someone tapped on my driver's side window. Raul stared me in the face. His hair was slick with product, and he always wore a bomber jacket. He was a middle-aged Danny Zuko with a snarl and a gut.

I rolled the window down.

He leaned closer, nodding to Irene. "Miss Macdonald."

Raul always was polite.

She returned his nod. "Raul."

"Horace thought you might be with Ortiz. Said you'd do it just to fuck with him."

She flashed a pained grin. "You can tell him I have better things to do with my time than piss him off."

Except she apparently didn't. I was just another in a long list of choices meant to poke at Horace.

"You can tell him yourself." The gun in his shoulder holster was close enough for me to grab, but he didn't worry about that. Why would he?

His gaze fell on the staff in Irene's lap. His eyes glazed over, like trying to absorb something he couldn't quite see.

"Are you going to kill me right here?" I asked.

The question returned his attention to me. "What? You think I can't?" He waved to a cop helping to supervise the cleanup. "Hey, Harold. How's it going?"

"Crazy day," replied Harold, turning his back on us.

"Horace has half the cops in his pocket," said Raul. "I could rent out a stadium and shoot you in front of a live audience and nobody would give a damn. Now get out."

He herded me into the back seat, shoving the golf bag to one side. He gave the bag the same unfocused stare he'd given Irene's staff before shaking it loose and taking the driver's seat.

I said, "If you kill me, you won't get the money back."

He glared at me from the rearview mirror. He didn't pull his gun. We all knew it was there.

"Oh, I think we'll find it," he said. "Like maybe in your apartment. Like maybe behind your couch."

Irene grumbled. "Damn it, Ortiz. How did you manage to steal that much money in the first place if you're such a terrible criminal?"

"Even the stupidest monkey stumbles across a banana now and then," said Raul.

"I didn't think I needed to hide it anymore." I put my hand on the golf bag. "I thought I was protected."

Raul said, "Now I'm going to drive, and if you try anything I'll shoot you. And if you somehow manage to get lucky and not get shot by me, that green car right behind us is going to follow us, and one of the guys in it will shoot you."

Raul drove away, giving us one last parting glance at the mess. The Dragon had left paw prints seared into the pavement, but if someone wanted to ignore them, they could always pretend they were potholes in a peculiar pattern. The green car followed right behind.

Irene turned to me in the back seat. "So why are we letting Raul drive us around like helpless little sheep?"

"I don't want to hurt him," I replied.

Raul chuckled. "Very kind of you."

"Well, aren't you a humanitarian, Ortiz," she said. "You know that he's going to try to kill you eventually?"

"Not necessarily," I said.

Raul had a good laugh at that.

I leaned forward. "If you don't let us go, we can't be responsible for what happens. The only reason I haven't tried to escape is because there are a lot of people around right now, and I don't know how any of this shit really works."

"Thanks for the warning."

Irene said, "Okay, so don't believe him. But what happened to Roger and Bill and Dwayne? If Ortiz is so harmless, how do you explain that?"

His brow furrowed as he cast a glance in the rearview at me. "Maybe he paid them off. Maybe they were in on it with him."

She shook her staff. Even if he didn't think I was dangerous, a weapon was a weapon.

"How do you explain this?" she asked.

"I don't have to explain shit."

That ended the conversation. We sat in silence.

We drove to the farm. I knew the way. I'd been there a few times.

The farm sat thirty minutes out of town. It wasn't much to look at. Just an old farmhouse, a barn, and a few acres of woods. There was a shack in those woods where people who displeased Horace sometimes ended up. They never came out alive, and rarely in fewer than three pieces. It was miles from the nearest neighbor.

It was perfect.

Raul drove up the gravel driveway, past the decaying farmhouse, pulling the car into the rundown barn.

"Get out," he said.

I grabbed my golf bag, and he didn't seem to mind. Didn't say anything about Irene's staff either.

The guys in the car that had followed us approached. They were big and intimidating. Buster wore a suit a size too small for him.

Probably on purpose to emphasize his muscular frame. Ray wore a turtleneck and nicely creased slacks. I'd never seen him not wearing designer aviator sunglasses.

"Okay, we can work this out," I said. "You keep the money. Give it back to Horace, say you couldn't find us. He'll be happy."

Raul shook his head. "Horace won't be happy until you're dead." He tossed the money to Ray. "Let's be honest. He won't be happy even then. But he'll be less unhappy, which is as close to happy as he ever gets."

They led us toward the shack.

"What's the deal?" asked Irene. "Are you going to kill Ortiz here? What about me? Horace finally decide I'm more trouble than I'm worth?"

"She didn't have anything to do with it," I said. "It was all my plan."

"Why are you bothering?" she said. "These guys can't touch us while we have these things, right?"

I would have said yes when first getting the sword, but Leo was dead now. Carrying the staff hadn't saved him. The Dragon had killed my chosen champion. Whatever the rules were, I couldn't figure them out.

"I thought maybe I was being chivalrous."

"You're a real gentleman," said Raul. "You can breathe easy, Romeo. Horace just wants her to watch."

"That's sick," she said.

"Said he thought it might teach you a lesson. Plus, once word gets out about what's coming to your boyfriend here, it should keep any other guys from getting ideas."

We walked into the overgrown woods and arrived at the shack. It was straight out of a B-grade horror movie with its rotting timbers and rusted door. The decor was intentional. Horace didn't send someone to the shack unless they'd really screwed up, and he wanted them to know they'd screwed up in the last hour or two of their life.

I'd only been to the shack in the cleanup stages. I'd seen enough from that to have nightmares. I'd found most of the pieces of the last job, though it was only later that I realized his glass eye had been lost somewhere along the way. If I'd been a more responsible minion I'd have gone back to look for it, but it wasn't in my trunk, and I damned sure wasn't going back to the shack if I could avoid it.

But here I was again.

Inside the shack, there was a modified dentist's chair complete with straps to keep the occupant from wiggling too much. Tool benches ran along the walls. Raul opened one of the benches, sorting through the sharp things within the drawer.

"Stand over there," he said to Irene. "Not too close, now. You don't want to get wet."

Buster and Ray began unfurling clean plastic tarps across the floor.

"Jesus, you're a sick fuck." She turned to me. "Do you really give a shit if this guy gets hurt, Ortiz?"

Raul opened a drawer and picked through the various implements of torture with a frown.

"My opinion is evolving," I admitted.

"The bad news is that Horace wants this slow, so it's going to be slow. The good news is there's a ball game I want to catch tonight, so it won't be as slow as I could make it. Unless you give me any more lip. So shut the fuck up, and sit down."

The chair was surprisingly comfortable. Ray strapped me down. The universe didn't object. I guess it had its own plans.

I hoped it had its own plans.

Irene stood in her corner, eyeing the preparations. "How sure are you about this protection stuff, Ortiz?"

"Pretty sure." I did not sound as confident as I wanted to.

Raul placed gruesome instruments on a rolling tray. They were all clean and sharp and ready to use.

"It'll be fine," I said.

Raul hung his bomber jacket on a coatrack and slipped on a surgeon's smock. "I got to say, Ortiz, that I expected you to be whining like a little bitch by now."

"Would it help?"

"Never does. Doesn't stop guys from pleading and crying and trying to cut a deal." He held up a long, curved blade. "Do you really love her?"

"Yeah, I think so," I said.

"How about you?" he asked Irene.

She shrugged, mumbled something.

"That doesn't sound like a yes to me," he said.

"I don't know." There was a long pause. "Maybe."

The bad guys all shared a laugh.

"It's really shitty of you to put me in this position," she said.

"I'm a shitty guy. So how does that make you feel, Ortiz? You're about to go through hell, and she can't even lie about loving you."

"Doesn't feel great," I said.

Irene grumbled. "Maybe I'm too fucked up to love him."

"Plenty of fucked-up people love each other. Ray's wife is a real head case. No offense, Ray."

Ray shrugged. "I'm not so stable myself."

"See? But they've been together . . . what . . . four years now?"

"Five," said Ray. "She's a crazy bitch, but I love her."

"If there's hope for Ray, there's hope for us all," said Raul. "Well, not you two."

"So what? I'm supposed to lie?" Irene asked.

"It would've been the decent thing to do. Give the poor schmuck something to hold onto in his final hours."

"I'm just being honest," she said.

Raul lowered a plastic visor over his face and tested a small electric saw. It whirred with ominous intent. "Now I kind of do feel bad about this."

"Yeah, well, for what it's worth," I said, "whatever happens next, I'm sorry about that, too."

He smiled. "I appreciate that, Ortiz. I really do."

He picked a scalpel off the rolling tray and took a step toward me. He tripped on something. It was only a small loss of balance, but he reflexively steadied himself on the tray. It slipped out from under him, and the tarp under his feet shifted. He fell on his face in a classic pratfall. Several of the instruments tumbled down on top of him.

Ray and Buster laughed at his misfortune.

Raul rose to his feet. "Goddamn."

"Oh." Irene gasped. "Oh, no."

"What?" He wobbled a little on shaky legs as everyone in the room gaped. "I'm fine."

His hand went to his throat. He pulled it away to see it covered in his own blood.

"What the fuck?"

His speech was slurred. One of those pointy things had cut him badly across the throat. I didn't see how he was still standing, considering how quickly the red stain was spreading down his chest. He started spitting up blood in a gruesome gurgle.

"I'm sorry," I said.

In his waning moments of consciousness, he must have decided to take me out with him. He fumbled under his smock, pulling a gun. He half-raised it toward me before finally succumbing to weakness.

"Fuck you!" he spurted. Or so I assumed. It was hard to tell under all the gargling.

He raised the gun halfway before surrendering to his blood loss. As he fell, he mustered the will to pull the trigger once. His wild, flailing shot was in completely the wrong direction. It hit Ray in the shoulder.

"Damn it!" Ray clutched the wound.

Buster just stood there, looking at my golf bag with an all too familiar lust.

Ray checked on Raul, who was still sputtering a little.

"Fuck this. I'm just going to shoot this asshole."

Before Ray could get his gun, Buster pumped several bullets into his back. Three would've easily done the job, but he emptied the clip, reloaded, and put another two in Ray's head.

"Jesus," said Irene.

"He wanted the sword!" snarled Buster. "But it's mine!"

"You don't want it," I said.

He loosened his tie. "I need it."

"Okay. Sure. You can have it."

Buster's rage softened. "Really? You'll give it to me?"

Irene said, "Is that a good idea?"

He whirled on her. "Shut up!" His gun hand trembled as sweat glistened on his forehead. "You can't have it!"

"Let's stay calm," I said. "You'll untie me, and I'll give you the sword. Then we can all just walk away. Nobody has to do anything stupid."

"Yeah. Yeah. I'll untie you. That's the deal, right?" He worked on the straps with one hand, unwilling to put down his gun. It was slow going.

Irene pushed him aside. "Let me do it."

His eyes darted between me and the sword. He was like a junkie waiting to tie off.

She released me, and I nodded toward the sword. "You can have it now."

Buster threw aside his gun and snatched the sword from the golf bag. Gleefully, he threw open the door and bolted into the woods. He didn't make it far.

The evening sky lit up as a fireball struck him from on high. He didn't have time to scream before being incinerated. The sword and a smattering of smoldering tree branches tumbled through the doorway before a forceful wind slammed it shut.

"That was a lot." Irene picked up a flaming twig and used it to light a cigarette. "I think that sword is broken."

I noticed something next to Raul's foot that had caused his slip.

"What the hell is this?" she asked.

"Glass eye."

"Where did it come from?"

"Long story."

The shack door opened. A tall woman entered. She had a body made of polished stone, wrapped in a flowing satin dress that came off one shoulder. Rows of glittering beads formed her hair, and her shiny onyx eyes mesmerized me for a moment.

She smiled, and her beauty overwhelmed me. It was like looking at the first perfect woman. Every other human was just a dollar-store knockoff.

She took in the carnage within the shack, but her face remained serene.

"We should talk."

CHAPTER NINE

"I'm Anaya," she said. "I bear the jar."

"I'm Ortiz," I replied. "I bear the sword."

She nodded. "I've heard."

Irene elbowed me aside, breaking the spell Anaya had over me. Mostly.

"This is Irene," I said.

Irene thrust the staff aggressively at Anaya. "I've got the staff."

"Leo's dead," I said.

"A bearer has never died a violent death," said Anaya. "A thing like that sends shockwaves throughout the Dreaming World. All the bearers felt it. I only hoped he had time to find a worthy successor."

She appraised Irene. Her judgment was a soft smile. Either approving or amused or both.

"Come with me." She walked out of the shack. The expected light of dusk had been replaced by a soft golden glow.

I moved to follow, but Irene grabbed my arm. "Can we trust her?"

I shrugged as I walked after Anaya.

"Goddamn it," said Irene as she jogged alongside me.

We walked into a forest different than the forest surrounding the shack in the Waking World. The door was framed by an arch of vines. The knotted wood of the door looked as if it had been grown, not made.

A big hint was a butterfly the size of a dog fluttering among flowers. Those flowers had arranged themselves by color, turning to follow as we walked.

"Aren't you scared?" asked Irene. "Hanging out with us hasn't been good for many people's health."

Anaya spoke without looking back at us. "Death comes in its own time."

"That's not an answer."

"No, it isn't." Anaya glanced over her shoulder at Irene, and there was no mistaking the approval in her smile this time. "Perhaps Leo chose wisely."

The deeper we went the more lush and primordial the forest became. The giant trees spread their leafy branches to the sky. A bee as big as a condor buzzed overhead. I felt so small; but also, this world opened up for us. The trees allowed just enough light to keep us warm. The flowers parted in a welcoming path. A rainbow butterfly landed gently on Irene's shoulder. Its bright blue eyes shimmered with gentle joy.

Annoyed, she brushed it off.

"Where the hell are we?" she asked.

"The Garden," said Anaya. "Where the Gorge has endless hunger, this is a place of endless bountiful giving. You wouldn't normally be allowed here, Ortiz. Monty never set foot in it. The sword is too opposed to it, but I've opened the door for you so that we may talk undisturbed."

She reached up, and a tree branch lowered, sprouting an orangish fruit and dropping it into her hand. "White star apples. I've loved them since I was a child."

Other branches offered us apples of our own.

Irene measured the fruit. "Should we be eating these?"

"Knowledge of good and evil?" Anaya took a bite with a wry grin. "Seems a bit late to keep that from getting out."

"I don't even like apples," said Irene.

A multitude of fruits, vegetables, and other offerings grew along the branches.

"Grapes don't grow on trees," said Irene as she plucked a bunch.

I harvested a bag of Fritos. "Dreaming World logic."

The bag opened with no fuss, and I tossed a handful of corn chips into my mouth. They tasted amazing. These were the Fritos made by Centeotl and Huixtocihuatl, the gods of corn and salt themselves. So good that taking a bite taught me the names of those gods.

The Garden opened into a glen. Squirrels the size of wolves bound in the fields. The sun lowered itself just below the tree line.

Three mossy rocks sprang forth in a circle from the earth, and Anaya had a seat on one. She gestured for us to sit on the others.

We sat there as she closed her eyes, enjoying the melodious songs of birds. It felt wrong to disturb her.

"So what's the deal?" asked Irene impatiently.

Anaya said, "I'm here to offer you my own counsel."

"Leo tried to counsel me," I said. "It didn't work out great for him."

"Things will work out." Anaya smiled, full of peace. "One way or another."

The sentiment comforted me. She wasn't wrong.

"What the hell does that even mean?" asked Irene.

The edge in her voice drained every bit of zen out of me.

Anaya said, "In the end, we must accept the capricious whims of the universe."

"I don't accept that," said Irene.

"One day you'll realize the universe doesn't care what you accept."

Irene grumbled.

"We are confronted with unknowns," said Anaya. "You carry that sword, and now, she carries that staff. These are things that should never have come to pass. This isn't your fault, but it's proof that even with a hundred lifetimes of experience events may be surprising. But we believe that the sword you carry, while it may not save us, can at least buy us some time."

"I tried giving it to someone," I said. "Two people, actually. They're both dead."

"The Dragon killed their asses," added Irene.

"Then you must have given it to the wrong people," said Anaya.

"Or the sword doesn't work anymore," said Irene.

"If the sword doesn't work then there's nothing else to be done, but the boons function by their own whims. It's more likely you've failed than the sword has. The sword is a tool, and a tool is only as good as the person who uses it. You must give it to the right someone."

"I need to find a swordsman?"

"Or swordswoman," said Irene.

"You are being too literal." Anaya waved her hand, and a jar appeared in the middle of us. "You've heard the story of Pandora, I assume. There is a kernel of truth, but what the jar carries and what it releases were not predetermined. It is the person who manifests what it contains and what it releases. In the right hands, miracles are let loose into the world and disasters are kept safe within. When chosen wisely, compassion and empathy and joy were set loose. Oh, and butterflies. Who doesn't like butterflies?"

"Doesn't really sound like miracles," said Irene.

Anaya said, "Doesn't it? The world turns on such small things. Not every boon is as destructive and obvious as your sword.

"But, more often, we've given it to the wrong person. My predecessors and I tried only to pick the best, most hopeful bearers, but nearly everyone has something ugly and unpleasant deep within. They might never act upon it. They might be the nicest people you will ever meet, but they open the jar, and it draws on that secret ugliness, sending it out to infect the world. Hate and war and pain. And that itch on your back you can't quite reach but that you can't quite ignore."

"I hate that," I said.

"That's the nature of the boons. They don't give us what we want. They give us what we are. Humanity isn't ready. Perhaps it never will be. Every bearer realizes that sooner or later."

"That's why you hid away and stopped bestowing them," I said.

"Yes, but now I suspect that this was no solution at all. The boons want to be used. They need to be used. Without them, humanity was left adrift, uncertain of itself and its purpose. That's something else the boons do. They give purpose. It's we bearers who are meant to guide that purpose. We abdicated that responsibility, and now we are paying for it. I pray that the whole universe doesn't suffer for our mistakes."

A shadow fell across the Garden as something massive passed over the treetops, blotting out the sun. A hot breeze blew through the glen, and I was slightly uncomfortable. In the beauty of the Garden, it was like getting hit by a blizzard.

"He's coming," said Anaya.

"It's me," I said. "You said it. I'm not supposed to be here. Monty and I are connected. He'll find his way here if I stay."

Anaya smiled. "He already has."

A bright light slithered from out of the edge of the clearing. Its tendrils dragged it forward. An ancient tree, possibly older than the universe itself, swayed as its impenetrable bark cracked and flaked. The brightness dissolved, leaving Monty in its place.

"I wondered if you would dare step foot here," said Anaya.

"It hurts." His body of light flickered, as if struggling to hold itself together. "But how could I resist?"

"I suspected you couldn't." Anaya nodded to him like an old friend. "You understand we thought the betrayal our only choice."

He laughed. "I'm surprised you called it that."

"It's what it was," she said. "You were a victim of that sword. If we could have come up with a better way, if we had been better people, maybe we could have found a way to save you."

"Nothing you could have done would've changed things, if that makes you feel any better."

She frowned. "It doesn't, but what's done is done. I don't know what happened to you in the Gorge, but—"

"And you can never know," he said. "It probably did drive me mad. Time becomes meaningless surrounded by that nothingness. I remember screaming forever into the emptiness. I think I still am. Part of me is convinced this is all an illusion, a shelter of madness. None of it is real."

"It's real," I said.

He chuckled. "There's a man with nothing but his own mind to keep him company for eternity. He hallucinates a flower, and as the eons pass the flower becomes more and more real to him. Until he can pluck it, feel its petals between his fingers, smell its sweet scent. Until, in the emptiness, there is nothing but him and the flower that he forgot doesn't really exist. How would he ever know what was real?"

"Yeah, yeah," said Irene. "Plato's cave. We've all heard it."

"I can think of nothing more poetic than beginning with this place, then." He reached for a flower, which twisted and shrank away from his touch.

"Is that your plan, then?" asked Anaya. "Revenge. Destruction until nothing is left?"

"I'm not a monster," he said. "The Gorge changed me, but I changed it as well. I've mastered it. I spent countless centuries burdened by that sword, but now, I see all the connections. I thought I needed the sword's power, but the sword is just a tiny sliver meant for mortal hands. I have bigger dreams."

"You don't have to do this," said Anaya.

He smiled, held out his arms. The Dragon's shadow covered the Garden. Its hot breath swept through the treetops, and the earth trembled.

The lid popped off Anaya's jar, and Monty bent toward it as if pulled by a gravity only he could feel. The Dragon roared.

"What the hell is this?" he grunted. "You can't use the jar."

"The rules are a bit fuzzy now, aren't they?" said Anaya.

"The Gorge couldn't hold me," said Monty. "What makes you think . . . what makes . . . makes—"

His body dissolved into sparks and lens flares. They swirled into the jar with a pop. Anaya gently placed the lid on it and set it back down.

"You used Ortiz as bait," said Irene.

"Opening the door to him opened the door to Monty. I suspected the chance to destroy the Garden would be irresistible, but I also suspected the Garden would defend itself. It used the jar to contain Monty like an infection."

"I thought the jar didn't work like that," I said.

"The jar works the way the jar works," said Anaya. "Like all boons, it's more of a set of metaphysical guidelines than absolute rules."

"What happens if he escapes?" I asked.

She fixed me with her onyx eyes. "You already know, Ortiz."

The Dragon screamed, and I covered my ears. The sound was deafening, but I was the only one who heard it. A leaf yellowed, fell from a branch. It circled in agony in the air before hitting the ground. Tiny cracks broke the Garden's soil, but they were like fissures tearing apart continents.

"He's going to destroy the Garden," I said.

"The moment you stepped foot in the Garden it was doomed," she said.

"You knew?"

She nodded. "A necessary sacrifice."

I'd screwed up a lot of things in my life. A lot of things. Maybe everything. But this was an unforgivable sin. I'd ended paradise.

"You couldn't have entered if I hadn't invited you," said Anaya. "It was my decision, not yours. The Garden and the jar contain him. I can't say how long. Guidelines, not rules."

"But you said the Garden was his opposite," said Irene.

"Opposite, but not equal. The Garden is endless bounty, but the infinite hunger of the Dragon is boundless. Once that hunger entered the Garden, it was doomed. There was no stopping that. But while Monty is contained and the Dragon distracted, you can find the right person to use the sword and restore order. If the Garden must be sacrificed to make that possible, then that's what must be done."

The jar rattled in place as a small crack appeared in it. Anaya turned her face away.

"You'll die with the jar," said Irene.

"Immortals confronting their own mortality." Anaya put her finger to the tiny chip in the smooth perfection of her cheek. "I'm at peace with it."

"Bullshit," said Irene.

Anaya laughed. "You'll make a fine sage one day. But that day will only come when Ortiz does what he needs to."

She plucked a seed from a tree and dropped it at her feet. The ground opened up, drawing the seed into it. A door covered in flowers sprouted before us. Anaya opened it to lead us back to the shack full of corpses.

"But what about the other bearers?" I asked.

"They may be useful," said Anaya. "But then again, they may not."

"Fuck them," said Irene. "They screwed this up. We don't need them."

She walked through the door.

"I don't know if I can do this," I said.

Anaya put a gentle hand on my shoulder. "No one has ever believed in you before, Ortiz. Not even you. And with good reason, I suspect. But circumstances have selected you for this, and who are we to argue?"

"Next you'll tell me everything happens for a reason."

"Close. Everything happens. What we do with that is up to us. Sometimes."

I tried to measure the pep talk against all the other pep talks I'd had in my life, but the only one I could remember was when my high school guidance counselor told me that the world needed garbage collectors, which when I thought about it was an insult to me and garbage collectors. It wasn't an easy job. Probably why I'd been fired from it.

"Now go. You and that unwelcome sword are destroying the Garden that much faster. And we will need all the time we can get."

She pushed me out the door, slamming it behind me. I opened it, but the Garden was gone. Just the decaying farm that should have been there.

I held the sword limply. It was so heavy, and yet I couldn't let it go.

Irene pushed her way past me. "Come on, then."

Dragging the sword, I followed her. She was more determined, more driven than I'd seen her.

"What are we going to do?" I asked.

She tightened her grip on her staff. "We're going to find a goddamn sage."

CHAPTER TEN

It probably said something about us that we were surrounded by thugs and murderers, petty crooks and lowlifes, but not a single person we'd consider wise. There was no rule criminals had to be stupid, but I didn't know any sage candidates.

We drove back to my neighborhood and went to the park. It was a crappy neighborhood with a crappy park. Some rusted playground equipment, yellowed grass, and a giant litter box masquerading as a volleyball court with no net. There were a few picnic tables, and the weather was nice, so some people were enjoying themselves. Others walked the sidewalk trail encircling the whole affair. We sat in a bench as Irene assessed potential candidates. She'd pick out the right person to unlock the full power of the staff. They'd give us the advice we needed.

Or they'd die horribly. Like the firefighter had when I'd given him the staff.

"Maybe we shouldn't do this," I said.

"What choice do we have?" replied Irene. "Neither of us know what we're doing."

"But after what happened with the sword—"

"That's the sword. You heard Anaya. It's not working right. But the staff should be fine. It will bring out the wisdom in someone."

"Anaya said the boons only work best when they're in the right hands."

"So I'll find the right person, then."

She said it with such conviction, I almost believed her. It might have also been that as the bearer of the staff she was taking on properties of a guide herself. It might have been because I was desperate and she was certain and I didn't have many other choices.

I pointed to a middle-aged woman power walking with purpose. "What about her?" I asked.

"She reminds me of my grandma," said Irene. "I hated my grandma."

I suggested a dog walker.

"No way. He didn't clean up after his dog."

"That lady?"

"With those shoes?"

"You're making this harder on us than it has to be."

"Us? When did this become an *us* decision?" She pulled her staff closer to her. "I carry the staff, so we'll trust my intuition."

"Was it your intuition that told you to sleep with me?" I asked.

"I slept with you despite my better judgment. Now that I'm paying attention, it should be fine."

She spent the next few minutes chewing an unlit cigarette as she took measure of candidates.

"Too handsome."

"Too full of herself."

"What's his fucking deal?" she asked of a guy whose biggest visible character flaw was perhaps loving jewelry too much.

"That guy looks okay," I tried.

"With that haircut?"

"I see that we're adhering the highest moral standards."

"Choosing that haircut is a moral failing. Now let me do this."

She decided on a woman with several rowdy kids. The kids ran off to the playground like a pack of hyenas while the woman, looking thoroughly exhausted, leaned against a lamppost.

"That's the one," said Irene.

"Why her?"

"Look at her. She's a mom. Moms are wise."

"My mom wasn't wise," I said.

"Just trust me."

The woman raised her tired head as we neared.

"Here." Irene held out the staff. "This is for you."

Irene feigned confidence, but she hesitated to hand the staff over. The woman took it without questioning, and I thought this could work. But I stepped back just to avoid whatever fallout might come. The woman took the staff. She straightened, appearing taller and more authoritative. A light came into her eyes. In that moment, she saw truths beyond understanding and glimpsed unknown secrets.

"Oh no," she said. "I do not need this shit today."

She tossed the staff back at Irene, collected her kids, and dragged them out of the park as fast as she could.

"Disappointing," said Irene, "but it didn't kill her."

Emboldened, Irene picked an old man sitting on a bench. Old people were wise, she reasoned. She offered him the staff, which he took tentatively.

He started screaming as he cried tears of blood.

Irene yanked the staff away, and he fell catatonic. Slumped on the bench, he stared straight ahead without blinking.

"Damn it, I think this one we did kill," she said.

"We? Since when did this became a *we* decision?"

She shook him gently by the shoulder, and he snapped to attention. A vague confusion crossed his face as he stood and shuffled away as fast as his tired old feet could carry him.

"This is frustrating," she said. "Let's think about it. The boon and the recipient are like two halves of a whole. The staff grants guidance, but it has to be the kind of person who fits the role. Maybe it's an archetype. Symbolism."

"What the hell does that even mean?" I asked.

"We gave the sword to a firefighter, but firefighters aren't fighters."

"Fighter is in the name," I said.

"Sure, but that sword is violence. It brings out the inner rage and ambition of the user. For the staff, what we need is someone who is wise. Someone like Merlin. Old. Mysterious. Bit of a curmudgeon. We need a wizard. Or a witch. Even better."

"A witch," I said. "Like an old crone?"

"Could work," she replied. "I don't suppose you know any?"

I knocked on Mrs. Cuervo's apartment door. Hard.

"She doesn't always answer on the first or second try," I said.

"Shut-ins don't seem like fountains of wisdom," said Irene.

"She's not a shut-in. She just keeps to herself. And isn't that part of the thing? The wise old elder that lives atop the mountain?"

"We're two doors from your apartment."

"You're the one who said it was symbolic, not literal."

"Two doors," she repeated.

"Obi-Wan lived on the same planet as Luke, just a couple of miles away."

"That's a foolproof argument."

"We'll just try it." I knocked on the door.

"How do you know she's even home?"

"She's always home."

"Sounds like a shut-in to me." Irene put her ear to the door. "I can only hear a TV. I bet your sage died a week ago. Her cats are eating her."

"She doesn't have cats," I said.

"She has cats," said Irene.

"You've never even met her."

"I'm just playing the odds."

I knocked again. Louder. Longer.

"This is a waste of time," said Irene.

"She'll answer."

The TV volume lowered.

"Mrs. Cuervo, it's me! Ortiz. Your neighbor!"

I banged the door for extra measure, but the door opened a crack mid-knock. "All right already. I heard you. I heard you." Mrs. Cuervo and her white eye scowled from the shadows.

"It's Ms. Cuervo."

The bent old woman snorted and nodded toward Irene.

"This your girlfriend, Ortiz?"

I nodded.

She passed silent judgments. Silent except for the smacking of her lips and a whistle from her nose. "What do you want?"

Irene stepped forward. "I wanted to give you this."

She made a halfhearted offer with the staff. Ms. Cuervo took measure of the boon. She didn't grab it right away. She thought about it first. That was wise, wasn't it?

She folded her bony fingers around the staff, and unlike the others, there was no change in her. She remained exactly the same.

"Well, haven't you two ended up in the middle of a great big pile of doodie? Don't just stand there. Come in already. And close the door behind you. You'll let my cats out."

Smiling, Irene gestured for me to go in first.

We followed her into her apartment. The place smelled of dust and layers of plug-in air fresheners. Sandalwood and sage and mint and pine and ammonia compiled in a stink that was more offensive than one might expect.

The blinds were closed and a single lamp and TV screen lit the darkness. Ms. Cuervo took a seat in a worn recliner in front of the TV. She turned it down, but not off.

"I'm not missing my shows because you two screwups don't know how to do your job."

There was no other place to sit. The apartment was mostly bare. Ms. Cuervo didn't do much beside sit in her chair and watch TV. I doubted she even had a bed. Probably slept in the recliner.

The only other furniture was an elaborate cat tree against one wall where shadows dwelt. They studied us with a dozen unblinking green, orange, and blue eyes. Like Ms. Cuervo, they did not find us worthy of anything but disdain.

"You have questions?" she asked.

"What are we supposed to do?" said Irene.

Ms. Cuervo held up her finger and shook it. "Not you. Him."

"Why does it matter who asks the question?" said Irene.

Ms. Cuervo turned up the TV with a frown.

"Why would it matter?" I asked.

She lowered the volume. "She bears the staff. She's not allowed to use it."

"I'm not using it," said Irene. "You're using it."

Ms. Cuervo raised the volume, louder than before.

"We were told the boons worked more along guidelines than unbreakable rules."

Ms. Cuervo snorted.

"So I ask the questions," I said. "Got it."

Ms. Cuervo pursed her wrinkled lips and lowered the volume. "The Dreaming World has its rules. You don't think you can get around them with a technicality, do you? I shouldn't even be talking to you, but . . . desperate circumstances. An exception can be made this once."

"Okay, so who do we give the sword to?" I asked.

"You already know the answer," she replied.

"How is that helpful?" asked Irene.

"If she keeps asking questions I'll have to give her this stupid stick back. Good luck figuring out this mess on your own."

"I can't even express rhetorical questions now?" said Irene. Then, realizing it was a question, she scowled as she mimed locking her lips.

"She can't just tell us," I said.

"This guy gets it."

"Can I at least talk to Irene?" I asked.

"Sure. Brainstorm. Do what you gotta do."

She got up from her chair. It was a slow, awkward process, and she only managed it with the staff to help her. I couldn't imagine how tough it was without it. It made me appreciate that she was a stubborn old lady. Almost made me want to give the sword to her.

"I'm going to grab an Ensure. Have some better questions by the time I get back."

She hobbled away. Her apartment was as small as mine, but she was slow.

"I don't like her," said Irene.

"It's the staff," I said. "Not her."

"No, it's her." She eyed the wall of cats eyeing us as another fluffy shadow slithered between our legs. "Let's figure this out and get out of here. It's somebody we know."

"She didn't say that," I said. "She said we already knew the answer. That's not the same thing."

"Fine. What kind of person do you give a monster-slaying sword to?"

"A hero," I said.

Ms. Cuervo laughed as she pushed her way though and between us. "That sword isn't made for heroes. Excalibur, Halāyudha, the Lance of Olyndicus, those are all weapons made for heroes."

"Are those all real?"

Ms. Cuervo shrugged. She pointed to my golf bag. "The day that sword was found by humanity it found its way into the hands of a real mean son of a gun. The Dragon met its user on equal footing. Aggression, rage, endless hunger. Two hateful appetites bound together, and this is the way it has always been."

The answer hit me, and I knew it was right because I could feel the sword singing in my head. Screaming, really. Like a madman standing atop a mountain of corpses, covered in blood. It almost made me throw up.

"We have to give the sword to an asshole."

"You're on a path. Have to follow it to the end." Ms. Cuervo tossed the staff back to Irene. "Now get the heck out of here and let me watch my shows."

She sat back in her recliner and didn't say another word.

We let ourselves out.

"Who's the answer?" asked Irene, though I suspected she already knew as well.

"You aren't going to like it," I replied as the sword's joyful psychic howls started giving me a headache.

CHAPTER ELEVEN

"No way," Irene said. "No fucking way."

"It has to be Horace," I said.

"You are not bestowing supernatural power on that son of a bitch."

"You heard Ms. Cuervo. The sword always needs someone mean and hungry and destructive. Find a dragon to fight the Dragon."

"But Horace is awful. If you give him the sword who knows what he'll do with it?"

"I'll take it back," I said.

She said, "No, you won't."

"Yes, I will. It's mine. I'm the bearer."

Irene said, "That won't matter. Horace never gives anything up. He gets that sword, he'll kill you for it. And don't tell me he can't. If there's a way, he'll find it. And then he'll be like some kind of awful god. Can you live with that, Ortiz?"

"I've learned to live with a lot of things," I said.

"What if he uses that sword and turns into the next Hitler or Pol Pot or—I don't know, there's hundreds of these assholes throughout history. And you'll be making the next one."

"Horace is awful," I said, "but he's not a genocidal maniac."

"But he could be."

She was right. Horace had no scruples, no honor, no moral center. The only thing keeping him in check was a paper-thin social construct. A psychologist probably had a word for it. All the usual ones came to mind, but whatever he was, he was a monster with only a shell of humanity.

It made him the best choice for the sword, but it also made him the worst.

"I'll take it back," I said.

I saw doubt in her eyes. The power dynamic between Horace and me had always been one-sided. I wasn't the kind of guy to demand anything of him.

"It's my sword," I said.

Meanwhile, the sword's psychic glee at the mere thought of Horace was bouncing around in my skull. It was hard to concentrate. Horace would want the sword, but the sword wanted Horace just as badly.

I'd slept with Horace's stepdaughter. I'd stolen his money. I'd told him how much he sucked. I'd killed six of his guys now. His ego might have been able to get over one slight eventually. Two or three, he'd hold onto that grudge for a good long time. But put them all together . . .

I saw myself how he must have seen me. A little weasel who had become an itch he couldn't scratch. But he wouldn't stop trying. He'd never stop chasing me, never stop sending goons, never accept that he'd be better off moving on. A magic sword wouldn't change that.

I left Irene at my apartment. She argued with me about that. Not unexpected. Arguing was half of what we did.

"I'm going with you," she said.

"No, you're not."

"What is this? More chivalry?"

"Whatever happens, you don't want to be there. He's your stepdad. If I'm wrong, the sword will reject him, and you don't really want to watch what the universe will do to him."

"You're forgetting I hate Horace," she said.

"Hating a guy is not the same as wanting to watch him get pancaked by a meteor."

"When a meteor enters the ground it's called a meteorite," she said.

I took her hand. "Look. We both know Horace is a terrible guy, but you're not a terrible person."

"Flatterer."

"I'm just saying, watching the man who took care of you after your mom died get killed, no matter how bad he is, no matter how much you resent him, might be harder on you than you think."

"But if you're right, he won't die."

"That's worse," I said. "Imagine that he takes the sword and becomes some perverse warrior-king ideal. You don't want to see that. Hell, I don't want to see it, but I have to be there."

Irene produced an extended, exasperated sigh. Then she mumbled to herself as she lit a cigarette.

"So you're not quitting?" I asked.

"Ortiz, I swear to god..."

I was halfway out the door when she pulled me close and gave me a parting kiss. It wasn't much more than a peck, but it felt like it meant something.

I ran out of the building before I could ruin the moment.

I had time to think about what I'd say when I came face-to-face with Horace again. I debated whether trying to explain any of it or simply thrusting the sword at him, letting the universe sort it out. Seemed easier. But I had a habit of doing the easy thing, and it hadn't worked great so far. Getting a magic sword hadn't made it more effective.

When I pulled up to the gate of his house I was either signing his death warrant or empowering him to do god knew what. If this were the easy way then I decided nobody could blame me for taking it. I hadn't asked for the damned sword.

The goon at the guardhouse appraised me with a raised eyebrow.

"I believe Horace will want to speak with me," I said.

He had me get out of the car and patted me down for a weapon. He looked over the vehicle, found the duffle bag of cash. The golf bag drew his attention for a moment, but he didn't go for the sword. Content I wasn't a threat, he opened the gate and let me in.

Waiting for me at the house were Big Jake and Little Jake. Big Jake was not especially big. Just slightly taller than average. But Little Jake was a woman of average height. It was all relative.

The Jakes tended to wear nice suits, though Big Jake liked to spice it up by wearing a colorful tropical-themed shirt under his jacket. Today's theme was tiki masks. Little Jake liked to pop her collar like it was the '80s.

The Jakes bore a passing resemblance. I wouldn't have been surprised if they were siblings. Or maybe they were married. Some couples just had that thing. Or maybe they just liked working together. I'd never bothered to get the details.

Little Jake chewed on a toothpick. "Did you bring the money?"

I opened the trunk and showed them the duffle.

"Okay. He's in the study," said Big Jake.

They took the duffle of cash. I slung my golf bag over my shoulders and followed them in the house. I was distracted by my own thoughts for a moment, and when I looked up, they were gone. The décor didn't match up with Horace's place. Instead, it was that small room and that chair again.

The chair's simple runes pulsed with supernatural light. Something inside me wanted to sit in that chair. Something else knew it was a bad idea. I got the impression the chair itself was mostly neutral on the subject. It didn't want to be here either, but forces bigger than either of us kept drawing us together.

"I can't sit in you," I said apologetically.

The chair's runes faded. The door behind me, the only exit, opened on its own.

"Thanks. We really should stop meeting like this."

The chair did nothing, but I got the impression it wasn't amused. Might have been in my own head, but it was a magical chair, so who could tell?

I left the room, stepping back into Horace's house. The Jakes flanked me as if I'd never left.

They led me to his study, a big room full of books Horace never read. He sat behind an expensive desk. The blue-and-gold curtains framed him as he took a sip of an expensive liquor.

Big Jake gestured toward a chair of my own. I made myself comfortable as the Jakes took their place beside a bust of some dead Roman emperor. Julius Caesar, maybe. Or Caligula. That'd be more Horace's style.

He smiled slightly but didn't say a word. Just sipped his drink and stared at me.

"I have your money," I said. "It's all there. Don't suppose I can give it all back and maybe we can call it even."

Horace jingled his ice. "We both know that's not how this works, Ortiz. You stole from me. I can't let that go. People will think I'm getting soft. People think I'm soft, then all this goes away."

"Damn, you really do love all this Godfather mob bullshit," I said. "Nobody's going to give a damn if you kill me or not. I'm nobody. Just some dumbass who did little jobs for you. Your organization isn't going to crumble whether I live or die."

His smile dropped as he ran his finger around the glass rim. I hoped he'd give the order to have me shot right then. The universe would squash him and put him out of the running for getting the sword.

"What happened to you?" he asked.

I was taken aback. Horace wasn't curious about people. But right now, he seemed genuinely interested.

"It's complicated," I replied.

"I bet." He knocked back the last of his drink. "Do you want something? You're a beer guy, right? Little Jake, get Ortiz a beer. One of those imported ones. The one with the funny label. You know the one I'm talking about."

"I'm good, thanks," I said.

He waved to Little Jake, who went off to do his bidding.

"You're right," said Horace. "You're nobody. I don't need to kill you." The widest grin split his face. "But goddamn I really want to. I've been fantasizing about it."

He closed his eyes and looked happier than I'd ever seen him.

"Even thought about doing it myself," he practically sang.

For a solid minute, he daydreamed of all the ways he could end my life. Long enough for Little Jake to return with a beer. I pondered the bottle before deciding, what the hell? I took a drink, leaned back in my chair, and enjoyed the moment.

Horace snapped himself out of his reverie. "But then I started thinking. Here's this guy who has worked for me for years. Under the radar. Never gets in the way. Never causes a fuss. Not a guy I ever thought much of, but reliable enough.

"Then he screws my daughter and steals from me. That makes sense. Sex does weird things to a person. Fucks with their head, their common sense. Do you love her?"

"Yes." I was as surprised as he was that there was no qualifier in the statement.

He nodded as he poured himself another drink. He held out the glass, and Big Jake dropped a couple of fresh ice cubes in it.

"She love you?"

"She doesn't know."

"That's gotta hurt, huh?"

I shrugged.

"She's like her mother," he said. "Well, not just like her. Her mother was an angel. A beautiful soul. Delicate. Having her in my life, I felt like a fucking Disney princess holding a hummingbird in my hand." He shook his head. "You get what I mean."

"Irene's not delicate."

He laughed. "I'm not a nurturer. I did my best, but that's just what people say when they screw up. The thing is that her mom wasn't easy to win over. Had to bring out my A game. But she was worth it. If you really love Irene, you gotta do that, too."

He must've saw the incredulity on my face.

"What? Just because I'm an asshole that doesn't mean I don't love love. It's a beautiful thing."

"Just didn't expect wooing tips from the guy who is going to kill me," I said.

He got up and sat on his desk. "Who says I'm going to kill you?"

That surprised the hell out of me.

"Oh, I'd love to do it," he said. "But I'm not an idiot. Like I said, I've been thinking about you, Ortiz. You're the kind of guy who gets by by keeping his head down. I've seen tons of guys like that. And eventually, most of them get ambitious. They overreach, and then it ends badly for them. But you keep running into my crew, and somehow, you keep coming back. That doesn't happen. Unless something has changed."

His gaze fell to the golf bag beside my chair.

"It's that sword, isn't it?"

He licked his lips like a hungry reptile.

"It protects me," I said.

"No shit. But it isn't yours, is it?"

I grabbed the bag and pulled it across my lap.

"Oh, I'm not stupid enough to try and take it from you. That would be very bad, wouldn't it, Ortiz? But I don't need to take it, do I?"

He set his glass down, leaned forward. There was something different about him. Something I couldn't define. Horace had always been a stubborn man. Now he felt unyielding. He radiated the authority of someone who made demands of the world and knew the world would fall before him.

The house rattled ever so slightly. I might have attributed it to my imagination if not for the chandelier softly jangling.

I couldn't give him the sword. I saw that now. It didn't matter what a thousand sages said. It didn't matter if God himself stepped down on a golden beam of holy light and decreed it accompanied by a chorus of angels. Horace wasn't the kind of guy who should ever have what the sword offered. I'd find someone else. There had to be someone else.

I stood. "This has been fun, but if you get it, then you know it's best to let me walk out of here before this place comes falling down around your ears. You can keep the money. Irene and I don't need it. And you leave us alone, everything will be fine for everybody."

"Sit down," said Horace.

And I sat, almost against my own will.

He stood, a tower of strength. Samson in a nice suit.

"You're not listening. We both know you need to give me that sword so I can do what needs to be done."

Madness filled his eyes. No, not madness. Madness implied a loss of control. He was on edge, but he still had enough presence of mind to not try taking the sword from me.

A tremor shook the house, powerful enough to knock several books off the shelves and rattle the windows.

"It's coming," he said. "I can feel it. Can't you?"

I could. It was hot breath on the back of my neck, a rumble in my gut, a pressure closing in all around.

"How?" I asked.

Horace said, "Because I was made for this, you idiot. Because you may carry the sword, but I'm the kind of person who uses it. Give me the sword, and I'll kill this thing, drive it back into the darkness." He reached out. The mania in his eyes was gone, replaced with a sincerity I'd never seen before. "Give it to me before it's too late."

Outside, inside, everywhere, the Dragon roared. I thought another building was going to fall on me, but instead, the wall collapsed as a giant golden claw came through. It snatched up Big Jake and yanked him out. Somehow, his screams could be heard above the howling winds. But only for a few seconds before he fell silent.

The house shook, and the chandelier came loose. It missed me by inches. Bits of crystal went flying everywhere. I was untouched, but a piece struck Horace in the cheek.

"What the fuck was that?" asked Little Jake.

Horace wiped the bloody gash with a snarl. "That was Ortiz's fault."

"You need to let me go," I said. "The Dragon is connected to the sword."

Horace said, "That's why you need to give it to me."

The house rocked as a crack split the study floor. A heavy bookshelf came crashing down on Little Jake. She groaned under the weight, and then the glittering claws on the Dragon burst through the wall again and pulled the shelf and Little Jake away.

"It's trying to stop us," said Horace. "It knows that I can send it back."

Outside the window, the Dragon stalked around the house. I could only see a portion of it, but its endless hunger was undeniable and overwhelming.

"There's a way to the world, Ortiz. Guys like you were never meant to be in charge of anything important. It's guys like me, like it or not, who matter. You're just here to help me do what I'm made to do."

Maybe it was the earthquake or all the pressure I'd been under the last twenty-four hours. Maybe it was because he was telling the truth. People like Horace, awful as they might be, made things happen. People like me stood on the sidelines where we belonged.

Horace was a bad guy, but the sword wanted to be in his hand, and the Dragon didn't want that. The study wall collapsed. The Dragon's red and black scales glittered with a light of their own as it craned its long neck downward to peer into the room.

"Give me the sword, you worthless little shit!" shouted Horace.

And I did, almost against my own will.

The pressure in the air faded as the Dragon withdrew. Horace strode out of the house and toward the monster like a legendary hero.

I expected him to be killed like the last poor bastard I'd chosen. I wanted him to be killed. Something told me it beat the alternative.

The Dragon tried to crush him beneath its clawed hand, but with a single swing of the sword the limb exploded into dust. It swung its tail, but another sword swipe disintegrated the attack. The Dragon roared as it swept its talons. Horace launched himself over the strike like a goddamn video game character. He flew two dozen feet in the air and plunged the sword in the Dragon's chest. The beast burst like a cheap balloon with a brilliant flash and a clap of thunder that threatened to knock me off my feet.

Then, only quiet.

There were a few scraps left. Some scales swirling in the air. A smell of ozone and sulfur. Horace stood there with the sword and a shit-eating grin on his face.

"I told you I could do it," he said.

"Great," I said. "Now give it back."

He strode over to me and looked me dead in the eye.

"Fuck off."

"You have to give it back."

He walked past me into his ruined study, found an unbroken bottle of some liquor and took a drink right out of it. "Do I?"

"It's mine."

He wiped some sweat from his forehead and chuckled. "I think it's mine. And I think I'll keep it."

"I'll make you give it back." I did not sound convinced.

Horace took another swig, tossed the bottle over his shoulder. "Okay. Make me."

I moved to take it, but he raised a hand.

"You sure about that, Ortiz?"

I could feel the sword's pull, but it was in equilibrium. The sword belonged to me, but it liked being with Horace. It liked being used.

The house groaned as a piece of the roof fell, almost hitting me. It might have been coincidence. Might have been the sword telling me something.

"It all comes down to the difference between guys like us," said Horace. "Guys like you sometimes stumble into opportunities, but they always drop the ball. Guys like me don't. So maybe the sword goes back to you. Or maybe this house falls down on your head. Except I don't think it's a maybe. I think it's a fucking given."

He stood unafraid, confident where this argument would end.

"Yeah, that's what I thought." He chuckled. "Keep the money. Keep Irene. I'll keep the sword. Now get the fuck out of here."

I walked away with a duffle bag full of cash, leaving a magic sword in the hands of the worst person I knew, because Horace was a guy like him.

And I was a guy like me.

CHAPTER TWELVE

"You left the sword with him?" asked Irene.

"It's complicated," I said.

"Damn it. Horace was a big enough psycho without magic on his side. What do you think he'll do now that he's some kind of goddamn chosen one?"

"He's not chosen," I said.

"Yes, he is. And you're the idiot that chose him."

"Irene, baby—"

I tried to put a hand on her shoulder, but she smacked my knuckles with the staff.

"Don't call me baby. And don't tell me you don't feel it. I've had this staff for a few hours, and I can sense its grand purpose. These boons change destinies, create gods among men, create monsters. Except Horace is already a monster. So what kind of messed-up shit is going to happen if we leave him with that sword?"

"I don't think the sword wants to leave him," I said.

"So what? It's your sword, isn't it?"

"I don't know. Maybe not. Maybe mine. Maybe Monty's."

"That's it, then?" she asked. "You're just going to walk away and let Horace be Horace, except with cosmic power at his fingertips?"

"What do you want me to say? I never asked for the responsibility. Two days ago, I was just a jerk with some stolen money and a girlfriend who hates him."

I sat on the couch, and she stared at me blankly for a while.

"You think I hate you?"

"We both know you don't like me."

Irene mumbled something to herself. She thumped the staff on the floor with steady rhythm.

"Ortiz, Jay, I like you."

"We both know you only screwed me to poke Horace."

"That was part of it, sure, at first." She sat beside me, put her hand under my chin. "But I do like you."

"What do you like about me?" I asked.

She closed her eyes and sighed. "Oh my god. Are we really going to do this? Do you really need me to give you a list of reasons like some kind of compatibility quiz?"

"No, it's okay."

"Fine. Fine." She stood, drummed her fingers on the staff. "Just give me a minute."

I gave her three.

She said, "It's not easy, okay. Just coming up with something off the top of my head."

I nodded.

"Okay, smartass," she said. "You tell me something you like about me."

"What? Now?"

"You said you maybe love me, right? It shouldn't be that hard."

She gave me three minutes. I didn't come up with anything.

I said, "Are we just two idiots who sleep together and make each other miserable?"

She sat beside me again. "After mom died, Horace and I had never had a good relationship. That stuff gets in your head. You pretend it doesn't, but cruelty is like a disease. And Horace is full of the stuff." She looked into my eyes. "Am I mean?"

"Kids are mean. Adults are assholes." I put my hand on hers. "You're just rough around the edges. That's all."

She pushed me away. "Thanks."

"No, it's okay. I kind of like that." I pulled her closer with a smile.

"What?"

"I think that's what I love about you," I said.

I couldn't read her. Truthfully, I had always been lousy at figuring out what Irene was thinking. She was either going to kiss me or slap me.

"You're such an idiot," she said as she pulled me to the bed.

Irene and I had never made love. We'd screwed. Animalistic, but not passionate. Passion implied depths and vulnerability and joy. We were more like creatures driven by instincts, pushed by circumstances and bad habits and poor choices.

We didn't make love now. We weren't ready for that. But there was a moment, when I stared deep into her eyes and she stared into mine, just a moment, when I thought...

I don't know what I thought, and I could see that she didn't know what she thought either. And I felt like maybe under all our damage and flaws we might be able to figure us out. The moment passed, but we both still saw it, even if we didn't know what to do with it and were relieved to see it go.

We lay beside each other. We were not cuddlers, but I pulled her close, and she held onto me like we were a couple of teenagers who had discovered sex and love and were afraid it would slip away if they broke contact.

It couldn't last forever.

She slid off the bed. "Gotta pee."

She disappeared toward the bathroom. I lay there with an alien feeling in my gut. Maybe I was happy. I'd forgotten what that felt like.

"Ortiz, you need to see this."

I pushed myself up on my elbows to see the bathroom in my small apartment. It was ablaze. The conflagration should have filled the apartment with suffocating heat and black smoke, but none of it passed out of the bathroom. Everything from the toilet to the shower to the tile was half-consumed, but no more. The room existed in a state of burning stasis.

"Weird," she said.

"Yeah, weird," I agreed, like commenting on a cloud shaped like a dog.

She closed the door. "Goddamn, I really gotta pee."

"You could walk to the gas station," I suggested.

Grumbling, she started getting dressed. "What does the bathroom being on fire mean?"

I got up and put my hand on the door. It wasn't hot. Neither was the knob. I opened the door a crack and peeked in on the room, still burning.

"It doesn't have to mean anything," I said.

"Or it's because you gave the sword to Horace. It's an omen or something."

"It doesn't matter," I said.

She pulled up her pants, grabbed her staff. "When I get back, we're going to talk about this."

"Do we have to?"

"You can't ignore every problem, Ortiz."

"We can try."

She made it as far as the front door. She opened it and closed it just as quickly. "Well, shit."

I didn't need to be told what she'd found on the other side. Another blazing inferno.

"Maybe try the window?" I said. "It's not a door. Not technically."

She struggled with my window. I'd never opened them. Never even tried. I was pretty sure they were painted shut. After much grunting and yanking—and just before I decided to offer some help—she managed, only to swear at what greeted her.

"I'm using the kitchen sink," she said.

Sighing, I got up to look out the windows. The world outside the closed ones was the same rundown little neighborhood I called home. But the open one showed a city aflame. Two different versions of the same place.

I dared stick my hand halfway out the window. The air was a little warm, but the flesh didn't burn or blacken. I extended until my forearm was bathed in the searing yellow light.

Irene pulled me back. "What the hell? Are you crazy?"

"It didn't hurt." I held up my arm. It wasn't even sweaty.

We took a longer look out the open window. The burning world went about its business. Cars rolled along as if the street wasn't gooey tar and their wheels melting rubber. The humans, sacks of bubbling, blackened meat, carried about their lives without noticing.

Irene closed the window. Behind the glass, the world was identical, just not on fire.

"So what do we do now?" she asked.

"Wait it out," I said.

"How long will that take?"

I shrugged.

"We're supposed to wait here, in this shitty apartment, without a bathroom? And what do you have in your kitchen? Half a box of Raisin Bran and a carton of spoiled milk and fifteen cans of SpaghettiOs?"

"You forgot the pizza rolls. And I dumped the milk out this morning."

"We need to fix the door," she said. "Can't you open it to wherever you want?"

"I don't know. I never tried. Not on purpose anyway."

"So you have opened it to someplace else, then."

"Sort of," I replied, thinking about the room with the bad chair. "It never felt like I was doing it, though."

"You should try doing it intentionally."

"We could give it some time," I said. "I'd hate for something to go wrong."

She shook her head. "What could go wrong?"

"I could open a door to the bottom of the ocean. All that water comes flooding in. Or outer space, and we're sucked out into the vacuum."

"Can you do that?"

"I don't know, but now that's all I'm thinking about. Door into space. Whoosh. We're dead."

"Well, don't think about that."

"Hard not to, now."

"We're bearers. Protected by the universe." She pushed me toward the front door. "Just try opening the door somewhere else."

"Why don't you try it?"

"It's your door."

"So you admit you're afraid you'll do the outer space thing."

She said, "I admit nothing. Now open the door. And don't kill us."

I grabbed the handle, closed my eyes, and visualized the hallway that should be out there. Not the deep, dark void of outer space. Definitely not that. Anything other than that. Even the bottom of the ocean was better than that. But definitely not that either. And definitely not someplace with alligators.

"Well . . . ?" asked Irene.

"Alligators are from Africa, right?"

"That's crocodiles," she said. "But don't think of crocodiles."

I struggled to clear my head, but it wasn't easy. Nor was it entirely effective. "Give me a second."

I walked through that apartment hallway every day, but it was only a place to pass through. One of those places that wasn't important enough to pay attention to on your way to someplace else.

I recalled the water stain on the ceiling, the way the stairs creaked, the vulgar graffiti scrawled here and there on the walls. "Fuck off, Steven," was a personal favorite. I didn't know who Steven was, but I liked to imagine he walked by that message every day.

"Okay. I've got it."

I opened the door. The world of fire was gone. The ocean didn't come crashing in. Explosive decompression didn't kill us. There was a hall, though it wasn't the right one. The endless corridor stretched out in a checkerboard pattern of black and gray tiles.

"Where the hell is that?" asked Irene.

"I don't know. I've never tried opening a door to someplace other than it was supposed to go to before."

Something moved at the end of the hallway. It was so far that it was only a humanoid silhouette.

"Hey!" called Irene. "Hello!"

"Maybe we don't want to talk to them," I said.

"Who else are we going to talk to?" She waved her arms. Her voice echoed down the corridor. "We're bearers! Are you a bearer, too?"

The silhouette moved closer without saying a word.

"Oh, I don't like this." I started to shut the door, but Irene stopped me.

"We need answers."

"That guy's not right," I said.

The figure crossed the distance much faster than expected. He was a grimy, gray person dressed in rags. His long beard was wild and tangled. His eyes were small and black and menacing and hungry.

"Are you okay?" asked Irene.

The man glided closer. His posture grew more bestial. He snarled with broken, crooked teeth. He said something. Or maybe he just gargled nonsensically.

Cackling, he bolted forward.

I slammed the door shut.

"What the hell was that?" asked Irene.

"That's God," said Gwen from behind us.

We jumped. We were both on edge after the weirdo.

"Where did you come from?" I asked.

"Closet," said Gwen. "And that guy you found, it's always the thing any bearer finds when they try intentionally opening their first door to someplace else."

"That's God?" said Irene.

"That's what I think," said Gwen. "Trapped in the recesses of his own creation, driven mad by it. Or maybe he was always mad. It would explain a lot."

"Should we let him out?"

"I wouldn't. The way I see it, if it is God then best to just leave him where he can't cause any more harm than he already has. Anyway, you won't ever find him again." Gwen walked past us to the refrigerator. "What do you have to drink?"

"I gave the sword to someone," I said, "but I think something went wrong."

Gwen pulled a light beer from the fridge. "Did the person you gave the sword to kill the Dragon?"

"Yes, but—"

"Well, then everything is working like it should."

"The world outside this apartment is on fire," said Irene.

"Isn't it always?" replied Gwen.

Irene opened the front door, revealing a blazing hallway.

"Yeah, that's not great," said Gwen. "But the Dragon was slain, stuffed back in its box? This is the aftermath of its temper tantrum." She stepped outside. The conflagration blazed without touching her. "It's all impotent rage. Probably nothing to be worried about."

"Probably?" I asked.

"It's Dreaming World rules, which aren't really rules but guidelines. This never happened before, so I can't tell you what it means. Even if it had happened before, it could mean something different this time."

She came back inside, closed the door. "Give it some time. See if it clears up on its own. In the meantime, I'm here to extend an invitation."

She opened the door once more, revealing a sandy white beach and a pristine lake. Or that's what I imagined it would have looked like if it hadn't been burning. Even the water boiled.

Gwen walked out into it without hesitation, pausing a few steps to look over her shoulder. "Are you coming?"

"Where?" I asked.

She pointed to the shore as a glowing mist parted over the bubbling lake, and a boat pushed along by a cloaked figure appeared before us.

"To Avalon."

CHAPTER THIRTEEN

"Ah damn it," said Irene. "We're dead, aren't we? We died, and we're in hell, and that's why the world is on fire."

"You're not dead," said Gwen.

She walked toward the water.

"What's Avalon?" I asked.

Irene said, "I could explain it, but trust me, you want to go."

"Because you have the staff?" I asked.

"No, because I went to college. Avalon is like . . . Cybertron."

"Cybertron is a war-torn hellscape."

"Castle Grayskull for grown-ups, then."

She took my hand and pulled me into the fire. On this side, the door was connected to a small shack. It was the only building in sight of an otherwise unsettled place.

Gwen climbed into the boat. "Technically, you can use any body of water to reach Avalon, but I like this place best. It's normally quite beautiful."

On the far shore, the half-burnt trees blazed.

"That's Avalon?" asked Irene.

The Boatman spoke. He didn't have the voice of death. It was nasally. "Do you want a ride or not? I don't have all day."

We stepped aboard. He didn't do a damn thing, but his boat slid into the water. A thick fog rolled around us as the world disappeared. A serene quiet covered everything. You didn't notice how noisy the world was until it shut up. The boat silently skimmed across the smooth surface like polished glass.

The Boatman, his flesh clinging reluctantly to his skull, studied us with his deep-set eyes. If he had an opinion, he didn't volunteer it.

"Are we going to meet King Arthur?"

Irene's question broke the silence, both figuratively and literally. Sounds flooded in. The water rhythmically lapped in waves. The songs of birds came crashing down on our heads. The suddenness of it was an assault on my ears, but I adjusted.

"That's just a story," said Gwen.

"Just a story with magic swords and dragons," said Irene.

The Boatman smiled. His crooked teeth were like fangs. They'd probably fall out of his head if he tried to bite us, but that somehow made it more threatening. "I've known plenty of kings. I ferried that one away a long time ago."

"Wait?" said Irene. "Are you Charon? Because that's not Arthurian mythology."

"Mythology is a weird word to use when you're literally on a boat to a legendary land," said Gwen. "He's just the Boatman."

"I wouldn't say *just*." He turned his back to us. I was distracted by the faded tour dates on the back of his Anthrax T-shirt. "I'm the Boatman. There is one of me. There are thousands. In other places, do I drive the black carriage down abandoned roads? When a lost soul steps into the darkened wood, only to be guided out by a cloaked figure, is that me? Yes and no. I try not to think too much about it."

"You don't think about what you are?" said Irene.

"Do you?"

The fog parted just enough to allow a glimpse of the sun overhead. I put my hand in the crystal blue water, and it was warm and inviting. I could dive right in and swim to the bottom, welcomed by the beautiful spirits waiting.

"You won't come back," said Gwen, breaking the spell.

We sailed on. Fish appeared. Small ones at first. Then bigger, more colorful ones. But recognizably fish. I didn't know enough to name them. Then they became weirder. Ebullient piscine rainbows with giant golden eyes and fins sticking out in every which direction. They sang soft melodies that danced just behind my ears.

My mind expanded. I was using words like ebullient and piscine, which I was damned sure I didn't know. But they just felt right.

The Boatman became younger. His eyes shone with an inner light and all the mystery of him softened. The questions remained, but they didn't matter.

Irene leaned in and kissed me. She must have sensed it as much as I did. We were safe here. Maybe not forever. But for now.

"Ortiz..."

She put a hand on my face and looked deep into my eyes. And what she saw didn't frighten her.

The mists broke as the boat struck the shore. The Boatman, a cherubic youth in a Mister Rogers T-shirt, leaned into his pole.

"Everybody out."

"Just a minute," I said. "We need just a minute."

"You don't get a minute," said the Boatman. "Get out."

We climbed out of the boat and onto the beach.

The Boatman registered my disappointment. "Sorry, kid. I don't make the rules."

"Who does?"

The boat launched itself back into the water.

"You're not coming with us?" I asked.

"He doesn't get off the boat. He's the Boatman," Gwen replied as the golden mists swallowed him.

On the shores of Avalon, the world felt sharper, more real. It was as if I'd been living my whole life in a hallucination, and only now did I understand what reality was. I leaned down and ran my fingers along the grass growing at the edge of the sand. A purple flower twisted up like an eager puppy to meet my fingers. I thought about plucking it. But that would be sacrilege.

Irene held out her hand and a tiny bear with butterfly wings landed on her fingers. It reminded me of the Garden, a place I'd destroyed just by touching it. I stood, put my hands in my pockets.

"I shouldn't be here."

"A little late to change your mind," said Gwen.

She guided us through the forest. The place had initially reminded me of the Garden, but the Garden had been a paradise. Avalon was a fairy tale. Everything here was dreamlike and imaginary, which was weird given how much more real it felt.

Nothing in the forest matched in a traditional way. Every tree was its own unique species. A corkscrew trunk with red leaves grew beside a fractal group of branches with white and black flowers.

Fractal. Words kept sneaking in. I wondered if I'd remember them when I left.

A monstrous bipedal snapping turtle with massive tusks lumbered nearby. Several snakes, coiled like springs, bounced on their way.

A shadow fell across the forest. I thought it might be the Dragon, but I didn't get the same feeling in my gut. I stumbled into a clearing of lush greenery. The air smelled painfully sweet. A powerful stag emerged from the shadows. It radiated power and grace.

The primeval forest god looked down upon me with its golden eyes. It lowered its head toward me, but before I could touch it something touched me. I blinked, and the meadow and its god vanished.

"Don't get distracted," said Gwen. "This place is full of traps."

"Aren't we protected?" asked Irene.

"Not from this," said Gwen. "Wander off the path chasing a laughing bird and you'll never be seen again except as a flitting shadow just behind the trees. Drink that fresh spring water, forget everything and just sit there forever, like a mountain climber's corpse on Mount Everest. Except still alive. And for fuck's sake, don't step into any fairie rings, because I'm not going in after you."

We focused on the journey. Irene almost picked up a silver broach just lying on the ground, but I stopped her. In return, she kept me from getting distracted by a riddle carved in a stone tablet. The answer was swordfish. I was pretty sure it was swordfish. Maybe on the way back I'd stop and double-check.

The forest parted. We didn't leave it so much as it let us go. A towering castle came into view, as big as a mountain. Beyond its impossible size, it was made of shining, golden bricks, dozens of towers, and flags large enough to block out the sky. They all had different standards, griffins, dragons, shields, and maybe Jupiter on one.

We walked past the giant portcullis. Gwen knocked on a plain wooden door. It opened on its own.

"Once inside, we'll be safe. Unless you get lost." She stopped and pointed at both of us for emphasis. "Don't get lost."

There was more walking. Walking through long hallways. Through strange rooms with odd decorations. Each place would've taken hours to catalog, so after a while my brain started ignoring it. You've seen one titan's skull, you've seen them all.

We reached the throne room. It was fancy, but it wasn't as wondrous as I expected.

"Hard to conciliate with everything that came before," said Irene.

Gwen walked past the throne to a pool of crystal clear water full of colorful fish.

"One minute. She likes to make an entrance."

The fish swirled together in an elaborate dance, a dazzling blur beneath the water so fast that they blended together until they formed a single shape. The figure emerged from the pool, lithe and covered neck to toe in a glowing black gown. Her long hair swept down her shoulders, reaching to her waist. Little golden fish swam through it, disappearing and reappearing among the curls. Her face looked as if it had been sanded clean of features and wrinkles. Her eyes were small and dark and infinite.

Gwen introduce us. "Ortiz, Irene, this is Viv."

Viv, now dry, was taller than my first impression. Much taller. She glided forward as a golden sword materialized in her hand.

"Hold up," said Irene. "There's more than one sword?"

"Why wouldn't there be?" said Viv. "A sword has many uses, symbolizes many things. Mine represents courage, strength, and honor. Yours is one of rage, ambition, and threat."

"Is there more than one staff?" asked Irene.

"Probably."

"You don't know?"

"I could tell you what I know, but truth is elusive in the Dreaming World. Your mere presence here reminds us of that. You. And that sword."

She floated out of the room.

"She wants you to follow her," said Gwen. "She just didn't say so because she gets off on being inscrutable."

Irene and I ran after Viv as she strolled down a hall. Each massive window we passed overlooked a different world. Towering, futuristic cityscapes, boundless deserts, floating islands, undersea realms. I was distracted by a whalelike creature swimming through the purple clouds until her voice pulled me back to the moment.

"There is something about you two. Something . . . unexpected."

"Mom always told me I was special," I said.

"Did she?"

"No."

"What does unexpected even mean?" asked Irene skeptically.

Viv stopped, appraised me again for a long moment. She put a hand on my shoulder. Her delicate fingers felt like a vise, and she wasn't even squeezing. She made a clicking noise with her tongue.

"There are those among us who believe there is no grand plan, no special purpose. That bearers are chosen simply by chance. I don't believe that. Every bearer I've ever seen has been . . . better."

"Better how?" I asked.

"Do we really need to pretend as if we don't know what I'm talking about?"

She released me, and it was a frightening relief. Impossibly heavy and uncomfortable to be in her grasp, but now it was like losing contact with the earth itself, expecting to float away helplessly.

"Who the hell are you to judge us anyway?" said Irene.

"I'm the keeper of Avalon," said Viv with a smug smile. "Who the hell are you?"

She led us into a new room, a council chamber of some kind. There was a giant central table, constructed of a single massive circular cut of stone. It must have weighed tons.

"Is that the Round Table?" said Irene.

Viv placed a hand on the stone, traced her fingers in small circles. "It is round and a table. The importance you place upon that is entirely up to you."

Irene pointed at one of the chairs at the table. For a moment, I thought it was that chair that had been haunting me, but it was different. It was bigger and more elaborate than the others.

"Wait a minute. Is that Arthur's chair?"

"It was," said Viv.

"I thought the Round Table was supposed to symbolize equality."

"Arthur was a great man, but even he had his pride." Viv rematerialized her sword and laid it on the table.

"So is that Excalibur?" I asked.

"It is, and it isn't. Many names, many purposes. I have bestowed it to many through the ages. Arthur was just one. He was almost worthy of it. But his kingdom fell, and it disappeared from the Waking World. All that remained were shadows, half-remembered, glued together in stories. And a few bits kept here for as long as those stories exist."

She picked up the sword and kissed the hilt before sending it away. She started walking again, and we followed. We descended a staircase that I was pretty sure hadn't been there two minutes ago. Down we went until the walls became rough, opening up into a vast cavern. Dozens of torches flickered along the rock. We stood on a small overlook, and something stirred in the dark. I knew what it was, felt its quiddity in my bones. I stepped back.

"The Dragon."

The behemoth's steady breath rumbled up and over us.

"A dragon," said Viv. "You didn't think there was only one, did you?"

"This isn't the same one?" said Irene.

"It is, and it isn't. Many names, many purposes."

My whole body tensed up. If this wasn't the same dragon, then it was close enough.

"This one sleeps," said Viv. "Like Jörmungandr, waiting to destroy the world. Perhaps sleeping forever."

"How is that different than my Dragon?" I asked.

"Your dragon isn't asleep."

The monster in the dark stirred restlessly. It wasn't my Dragon, but it was a dragon. And it felt my presence.

"We should probably go before we wake it," said Viv.

We left the sleeping beast behind. Once outside the room, the pressure in my head eased. We didn't end up in the round table room, but I was getting used to doors following their own rules.

Viv said, "It's all intertwined. We bearers forgot that. We thought that by banishing Monty and the sword into the Gorge that we could remove them. But it didn't work, and now, I realize it never could have. Your sword is part of the universe. It can change. It can be one thing or many. But it exists because it must exist."

"This is all very philosophical," said Irene, "but what does it even mean?"

"Meaning is made, not found. Did the universe make the boons? Or did humanity? Some sort of semiotic symbiosis?" Viv smiled slyly. "Yes and yes. No and no. Such questions are irrelevant. Whether the mind gave birth to the boon or the boon gave birth to the mind, it all ends in the same place. But you've done your part, Ortiz. Your sword has been bestowed. Now we wait for things to run their course."

"But what about the fire?" asked Irene. "You can't tell me that's not an omen."

"Not really my problem," said Viv.

"Then why are we here?" I asked.

"Curiosity," said Viv.

She walked through a door, closing it behind her. When we opened it, it led outside to the enchanted forest.

"She does that," said Gwen from behind us. "Tour's over. Time to get you back home."

Another boat ride led us back to the burning world. Gwen opened a door to my apartment.

"We can't just wait here," said Irene.

"Trust me. In a few days, this will all blow over. Viv's right. You did your job. Nothing else to do."

"And what about Anaya?" asked Irene. "Is she dead?"

"Not yet. I'd sense if she were, but she is dying."

"Why can't we sense it?" I said.

"Too new. You get more in tune with the universe the longer you carry your boon." Gwen grabbed a beer out of my fridge. "How old is this pizza?"

"Couple of days," I said.

She shrugged. "I'm immortal. Should be okay."

She took a bite of cold pizza as she struggled to hold it and open the beer.

"Can she be saved?" asked Irene.

"No clue, but you're welcome to check."

She opened the front door to reveal the Garden. It wasn't on fire, but it wasn't looking good. A deep twilight covered the wilting trees and decaying flowers. A giant hummingbird flitted by, only to smack into a tree and fall to the ground, spinning in awkward, pathetic circles.

Gwen took a long drink and grimaced. "You should buy better beer." She threw the half-empty can into my already too full garbage. It rolled off the cans of SpaghettiOs and Twinkie wrappers onto the floor, make a small puddle.

"Good luck with that."

She went back to my closet.

"Wait a goddamn minute," said Irene. "You're not going to help her?"

"Me?" Gwen laughed grimly. "I like Anaya. I do. But I'm not crazy. Let the Garden die. Obscurities come and go. I'm not going to poke at it."

"So you just came to push that responsibility onto us?"

"Save the judgment. I didn't have to come at all."

"But we don't know what we're doing."

"Who does these days? All the rules have gone out the window." Gwen shoved the pizza in her mouth with a wave as she disappeared into my closet. I didn't open the door to follow. She was already gone.

Irene was thwarted from the argument she'd been spoiling for. I did my best to defuse the situation.

"It's okay, Irene," I said. "It's fine."

"It's not okay," she said.

"Yes, it is." I took her hand. "You can't fight every battle."

Frowning, she made a small attempt to push away from me, but I held tight.

"It's not right," she said.

"What can we do?" I asked.

An alien expression crossed her face. One I'd never seen before.

Uncertainty.

Irene might not know the right thing to do, but she'd always do something. But now, she was looking to me for guidance. And I did the only thing I could.

I shut the door to the Garden.

CHAPTER FOURTEEN

We could live on SpaghettiOs and pizza rolls. It probably had more to do with being blessed by the universe, but we managed for a week. When it seemed like a grocery run was unavoidable, we discovered the kitchen cupboard restocked all on its own. The refrigerator had the same deal when it came to beer, soda, and, occasionally, orange juice.

The bathroom remained an eternally burning disaster, but despite appearances, it worked. It was a little weird taking a shower. Especially since it still had the same problem with the hot water. As a true gentleman, I let Irene always have first crack at it, and she was never that long. But the water was still lukewarm by the time I got to it.

I turned on the melting sink faucet and ran my toothbrush under the water. The toothpaste bubbled from the tube. I brushed my teeth, studying my distorted reflection in the deformed mirror.

Irene opened the hall door. She checked the hall a lot. She closed it with a groan.

"How long does this go on?" she asked.

I shrugged. My mouth was full of toothpaste.

"How can you stand it in there?" she said.

The flames danced around me as I spit into the sink. The toothpaste sizzled and blackened against the cracked plastic.

"It doesn't hurt," I said.

"It's unnatural," she said.

"You've done it."

"Only when I needed to. You don't need to brush your teeth in there."

I reached for my mouthwash. "What difference does it make? It's just fire."

She sighed. "Yeah, it's only fire."

She'd stopped picking arguments with me. I missed the fights. They probably weren't healthy, but I missed her caring enough to have them.

She sat on the couch, turned on the TV. I sat beside her, took her hand in mine.

"It'll all be okay," I said.

She grunted.

This was pretty much all we did now. Eat SpaghettiOs. Watch TV. Not fight. Me and her in a shitty apartment, surrounded by an inferno, not talking. And I thought this might be how it would be.

Forever.

We watched TV for a while. She fell asleep on the far end of the couch. I put a blanket over her without waking her.

I washed some dishes. The discarded cans of SpaghettiOs and beer filled a corner. It wasn't space we could afford to give up in my tiny apartment. I threw it all in a garbage bag, debated on just tossing it out the window. Let it be someone else's problem. It was probably the wisest choice. I'd never been good at making decisions. It was how I'd ended up digging my own grave and finding that goddamn sword. And giving that sword to Horace was why I now permanently lived in a burning world. The fire might not touch me physically, but it had trapped me in this apartment.

"Screw it."

I threw the garbage bag over my shoulder and opened the front door. I strolled through the flames. While I was untouched by the fire, there was a stink to the world. I'd smelled it when opening the windows, but it was worse down here. The stench of burning concrete, burning flesh, burning metal and plastic. Burning everything.

I got rid of the garbage and on the way back encountered an ambling chunk walking a smoldering skeleton of a little dog. The skeleton sniffed my leg, and I bent down to pet it. Bits of hair floated in the air as it lapped at my hand with a greasy tongue.

"Cute little fella," I said to the humanoid chunk.

The smoldering flesh screamed something at me before carrying on its way.

I wondered if this was real or just the Waking World filtered through my connection to the Dreaming one. My best guess was that the two were connected, overlapping here and there. It was less either/or, and more about what level of reality I was tuned into. The Waking World was on fire, too. It was just more literal in the Dreaming one.

I walked to the corner store and bought some cigarettes. I'd trapped Irene in this dreary hell. The least I could do is get her some smokes. The meat that was the clerk gargled at me with his throat full of blood and bile. His blackened eye sockets stared expectantly at me.

"Those there." I pointed to Irene's brand.

He shuffled over, grabbed a pack, and slammed it on the counter. Bits of his flesh stuck to the pack. I picked it up in two delicate fingers and stuck them in my pocket. He gurgled something.

"Yeah, same to you," I said.

My shoes left prints in the melting concrete, and two mushroom clouds bloomed over the skyline. All around me the ruined Earth carried on, so I carried on. Hands in pockets, I skimmed across the apocalypse. It wasn't so bad if I kept my head down and ignored the stench, the warbling screeches of the walking dead carrying on conversations.

Back at my apartment, the apartment wasn't there. I opened the door to find the Garden. It was in bad shape. Its grass was brown. Its trees wilted and cracked. Bare patches of dry earth were exposed here and there.

I didn't care. I just wanted to get back to Irene and my apartment. I closed and opened the door again.

The Garden remained.

"No," I said.

Mrs.—Ms.—Cuervo's door opened. A thing shaped like her, if she were half-melted, shambled out. Ms. Cuervo never left her apartment. It was my first concrete evidence that I wasn't in the Waking World.

The thing moved toward me. Dead cats meandered around its feet. Some were more dead than others, but all of them stared at me with empty eyes. Ms. Cuervo, too. Except her dead white eye. It focused with sharp clarity, gleaming in her charred skull.

I closed and opened the door again. No dice.

Ms. Cuervo and her army of cats crept forward. I wasn't worried. The universe protected me. I was pretty sure it protected me. Though it hadn't protected Leo. It hadn't protected Anaya. But if the burning world didn't hurt me, then I doubted she could.

Ms. Cuervo moved within a foot and just stopped. She stared at me. Just stared. A cat rubbed against my leg. Bits of fur and skin clung to my pants. I did what I always did. I pretended like it wasn't happening.

Close. Open. Garden. Close. Open. Garden. Close. Open. Garden.

"Okay, this is really starting to piss me off," I said to Ms. Cuervo as I shooed away a cat.

Another corpse came down the hall. This one looked like a mail carrier. It trundled toward me, stopping a short distance away. It didn't try to touch me. Only stared at me in gurgling fascination. They made no effort to harm me, but the undead giving you the stink eye got old fast.

I opened the door. Garden.

"Goddamn it."

Another apartment door opened. I recognized the burning version of the guy I nodded at once or twice but had never talked to. It turned its misshapen head toward me.

Why had I left the apartment? Why did I think it would turn out any other way than this? Eternity with Irene and SpaghettiOs and TV wasn't great, but it beat the hell out of this. Whatever this was.

I shut the door, headed toward the street to get a little space, clear my head.

The lookie-loo undead didn't stop me. They followed me down the hall and to the building's front door. I wasn't surprised by what I found when I opened it. The Garden wouldn't be denied. No one would push me past that threshold, but I wasn't presented with many other choices. I heard the other apartment doors opening as more burning bodies came out of their holes. They wouldn't get in my way. Me and the dead trapped in this cozy between space. I pulled the cigarettes and thought about smoking one, just to kill the smell. As if it could.

I was an expert at the lousy deal. Sometimes, a lot of times, you just have to accept what comes your way.

I stepped through the door. The door withered behind me. There was no way back now. I followed the broken path to find Anaya sitting on a bench under the overcast sky.

She was in bad shape. Cracks ran through her stone skin. Bits and pieces had broken off, revealing grayed flesh and blood underneath. She looked up at me from her bench. Her eyes smiled.

"None of the others came," she said softly. The act of talking spread fissures around her mouth. "Yet here you are."

I didn't volunteer I hadn't had much choice.

"I bestowed the sword," I said. "The Dragon was slain, but I think it made things worse."

She smiled as if she might laugh but didn't. It probably would've caused her jaw to fall off.

"Why wouldn't it?" She cast a hard stare at the cracked jar. "We are fools playing with godlike forces."

She stood slowly. Brittle bits of her fell away.

"Maybe you should stay still," I said.

This time, she did laugh. A split ran across her jawline. "Your concern is touching, but we both know my time is coming to an end."

"Should you give the jar to someone?" I asked.

"To keep it from becoming lost? Perhaps it's better if it is, better if all these lousy boons are lost forever." She moved toward me, step by step. Her body cracked and popped as pieces fell off. "As long as these things exist, humanity is enslaved. We bearers thought to hide them away, but still, their influence can't be stopped."

She stood before me. The countless fissures on her face glowed with a familiar light.

I said, "You don't think that. It's Monty. He's corrupting you."

"Is he? Or am I finally seeing the truth? To think, I sacrificed myself in some vain hope of—"

Her onyx eyes went blank. Her mouth curled into a painful grimace. She fell into me, and despite being made of stone, she was so light and frail.

"Forgive me, Ortiz. I'm not myself."

I helped her back to the bench. Even the act of sitting caused her pain. She put a hand to my chest. The forearm was barely holding on to the rest of her.

"You're right. He's in here." She tapped her temple lightly, but the tip of the finger broke. Not quite falling off, but bending at an awkward angle. "Whispering. Clawing at my soul. But I can hear his secrets. Some of them. He can't hide them all."

The broken finger snapped off and fell into her lap. She studied it like a dead insect. Off-putting, but also, garnering some small amount of sympathy.

She took my hand, pulled me closer and whispered.

"He underestimates you, Ortiz."

"I don't know if that's strictly possible," I replied.

"Good. That's good. Humility."

"I'm not humble," I said. "I'm just an idiot who found a sword."

"Maybe so," she said. "But you're different than any idiot who has touched that sword before. Maybe that's only an accident, but it might all work out in the end."

An earthquake shook the Garden. Several nearby decaying trees were uprooted, splintering into pieces. Anaya screamed. Her right arm fell off, shattering into gravel. The jar teetered back and forth as its cracked shell burned with bright light. It was the jar shaking the Garden, not the other way around.

"The sword seeks a master. Monty wanted to be that master, but now, he wants more. That's the nature of the sword. It spurs an endless hunger for more." Teeth clenched, she seized me by the shoulder. "Tell me what you hunger for."

"Honestly, I'd like to just get rid of the damn thing at this point."

She shoved me away as uncontrollable laughter wracked her body. The quake tore away vast tracts of the earth, falling away into oblivion. It shattered the sky, leaving only darkness. Everything disappeared except for this patch of dirt, Anaya, the jar, and me.

The cracks spread across Anaya as she smiled warmly at me. "There might just be hope yet."

The jar disintegrated as Anaya crumbled away.

Monty stood in her place in all his glorious horrible gleaming beauty. Without clothes, he was more ethereal, more inhuman.

He stood over me on this tiny island of dirt, rock, dead grass, and one half-uprooted tree.

"Thank god. I thought she'd never shut up."

CHAPTER FIFTEEN

Monty stood before me, a glowing god of death and destruction. There was nowhere to run. The Garden was consumed, leaving only this small chunk of ground for us. All around, only emptiness and oblivion.

He held his hand out to me. I waited for him to fire a death ray from his fingers, melting me into a screaming pile of organic sludge.

"I'm not going to kill you, Ortiz."

"You're not?"

"We're bound together. Bound by the sword, the Dragon, the Gorge. Bound together in ways I don't completely understand yet. I don't know what effect killing you would have on me. I haven't figured out your place in this. Did you happen upon the sword by accident? Did it seek you out? Is it all chaos and confusion so unimaginable that our minds crave order, even when none is there?"

"Hell if I know," I said.

"That's what I like about you. At least you're honest."

He held out his hand again, but I waved it off.

"I'll sit."

There was no place to sit but the hard ground. That and a fallen tree trunk, but Monty took that.

He said, "So you bestowed the sword."

"Except I don't think it worked," I said.

"Why? Because the Dragon isn't truly dead? It can't ever be killed. It can only be temporarily returned to the emptiness from which it spawned until it grows strong enough to rise again. That's the endless, stupid cycle. That's the ultimate truth the Gorge showed me."

He smiled. His mouth flared. His eyes sparkled with pure golden light. He was inhuman, but so were the other bearers. They all carried these boons, and every one I'd met had admitted that they didn't understand them. I certainly didn't.

"I bestowed the sword, but the world caught fire after that," I said.

Monty nodded. "That'll happen."

"Is it real? Did I break the world?" I asked.

"You? No. It was broken long before the sword found you. Long before the boons came into existence. This was all set in motion when the universe was young."

"By who?"

"Whom," said Monty. "And that's the wrong question. If a boulder rolls down a mountain and crushes a mouse at the bottom, did the boulder do that on purpose? Did the mountain? Gravity? Purpose is only a thing we impose on the world. It's an illusion."

Our island of rock trembled. Something vast rumbled around in the dark below.

"The Dragon is restless," said Monty. "Always."

It was impossible to see anything in the darkness around us. It should have been impossible to see at all, aside from Monty's glow. But light clung to this little piece of Garden, unable or unwilling to go into the dark.

I said, "We're in the Gorge." The place was hostile, angry, but I was connected to it through that damned sword.

Monty waggled his hand. "We're more Gorge adjacent. I wouldn't worry, though. You're safe enough as long you stay here."

I wasn't close to the edge, but I scooched a few more feet away from it. He picked up a tree branch and threw it into the void. It sailed away, tumbling upward in erratic patterns before disappearing.

He said, "It wasn't always a sword. It first came to me as a spear. I found it by a tree, just propped there. I spent centuries thinking the nameless gods had placed it there for me. That I was chosen. It was a pretty big deal because back then, the gods were not to be fucked around with. Have you ever looked at the night sky?"

"Sure," I said.

"No, you haven't. Not like we looked at it then. It was beautiful, terrifying. We gazed at the heavens with awe and dread. We huddled by dying fires, just hoping that if there was something out there that it wouldn't notice us. We had a whole series of rituals meant to convince the universe to ignore us. Simpler times.

"When I found the spear I knew it was important. This was a thing that would change everything. I took it back to my people, and we pondered it. An elder tried to take it from me and was struck by lightning. Right out of the clear sky. I can still smell his seared flesh, hear his painful breaths. Lousy way to go.

"Some thought I was blessed. Some thought I was cursed. But my brother said it was a sign. The boon was a gift from the heavens, and he would use it to kill the beast that had been stalking us in the night. Just a little closer, every night. He'd kill it before it could kill us."

"The Dragon," I said.

"Cave hyena. So I bestowed upon him the boon, and I still wonder today if that choice is what set the rules. Like the universe was doing a test run, and it could've been different if I'd made a different decision. Drives me a little crazy when I ponder it." His eyes and mouth faded to almost invisibility in his face. "Crazier, perhaps."

He went on. "Filled with confidence, my brother disappeared alone over the horizon on his hunt. None of us had the courage to go with him. Not even me, who was protected by phantom lightning bolts. We assumed he'd die. All he'd do was give the beast a taste for us. Imagine our surprise when he returned, covered in blood and glory.

"We danced underneath those fearsome stars. We shouted our triumph with proud defiance. Like we had done something amazing. Like we had killed our cruel gods alongside that beast, and those primal spirits that remained would fear us as much as we feared them."

His whole body dimmed until I could see partially through him. There was a small pulsing light in his chest where his heart belonged.

"We didn't have a word for the devil, but a deal had been struck. The sword had the power to elevate humanity from the pathetic cowering things we were, but the universe responded."

"The Dragon."

"No, not quite then. That came later. Before that, my brother developed a boundless thirst for conquest. Many joined him, drawn to that spear. Others rose against him, seeking its power for themselves. It wasn't that humanity was peaceful before that, but the spear stoked the worst instincts, spreading like an infection. And I could only watch as the bloodshed threatened to consume everything."

"And you couldn't take the spear back," I said.

His body became more solid. "I tried. Several times, but I wasn't strong enough. You know how it works. You've sensed the sword's hunger. We might be its bearers, but we aren't its masters. It was mine to bestow, but once it had him there was nothing to do but wait it out. At the time, I thought the madness might claim the world, but I had no idea how big the world was. When I reflect on it now, it feels so small. Thousands dead and dying. The end of the world? A drop in the bucket.

"Just the same, it was awful until the fateful day he was finally killed. I'm not sure if the spear used him up or if it was simply inevitable. He didn't perish on a battlefield, drenched in blood and glory. He was poisoned. He died choking on his own vomit, surrounded by those who hated and feared him. He ended his life as a monster, not a savior, and it was my fault for giving him that spear.

"With his death, the spear came back to me. I wandered around for a long while after that. Met other bearers. We shared our stories, and we vowed to get it right next time, to find the right people and give them the gifts to make this world a paradise.

"But it was always the same. The world is broken, and the boons are broken as well. The other bearers retreated to their hidden corners. But the sword isn't for cowards. It wants to be used. It must be used. And I kept bestowing it. The results were always the same: blood and carnage, conquest, death. But after, a stronger humanity rose from the struggle. That's the truth of the sword. The world is terrifying. It lives on bloodshed. There is only predator and prey, and the sword ensured that humanity would be the predator."

"But then there's the Dragon," I said.

"The Dragon is the universe's response to humanity's growing power, but we have the sword."

I stood, brushed the dirt from my pants. I wasn't afraid of Monty. I couldn't say why. We were two of a kind in the end. Two people at the mercy of the unfathomable. "Leo said the sword screwed with your head."

"Without a doubt," said Monty. "How can anyone touch power

like that and not be affected? Maybe they were right to fear me. Maybe they were right to throw me into that Gorge. But it didn't work, and while I was there, I saw the truth. The Dragon will consume everything in order to stop humanity from rising. It will rise again and again until—"

"Until it finally destroys us or we destroy ourselves," I said.

He nodded. "Ah, I knew you'd get it, Ortiz. You're the only other person who could. You alone know that there's only one way this ends. That's the bargain I struck with the Dragon."

The Gorge shook as the Dragon lumbered all around us. Flashes of light outlined its titanic wings enveloping us. My scalp tingled, and a nervous twitch ran through my body. Fight or flight. Except this was all flight. Flight with nowhere to go.

Monty said, "I used to think all we could do was fight to the bitter end. Fight and die. The final fate of humanity to perish in a blazing funeral pyre to light the heavens."

All my life I'd been under somebody's thumb. Pushed around. Keeping my head down. He wasn't telling me anything I hadn't figured out before I'd ever touched that sword. I couldn't tell him he was wrong, but I wanted him to be.

"But enough about me. Tell me, Ortiz. Have you seen the Siege yet?"

Before I could answer, he smirked.

"Yes, of course, you have."

"I don't know what that is," I said.

"The chair. About yea high. Runes on it. Otherwise, pretty unremarkable."

"Oh, the Siege," I said.

Monty said, "I've seen it, too. I didn't have the courage to sit in it, and by the time I realized what it was Viv had hidden it away. If you ask her about it, she'll tell you it was for the greater good, but really, it was because she feared what it would give me."

"Leo said not to sit in the chair."

"Leo's dead."

"Because you killed him."

"Oh, Ortiz. And I thought you understood. Maybe I should just destroy you."

He burned brighter and moved toward me, hand outstretched. I wondered if it would hurt, but it was a clinical sort of wonder. The fear response I'd had moments ago was gone. All that was left was grim acceptance. Like a rabbit sitting in its warren, listening to the raspy breathing of wolves just outside. Nowhere to run. Nothing to do but wait for it.

Monty stopped. He looked at me strangely, as if he couldn't quite see me. "No, not yet. Not yet."

He walked to the edge, peered into the darkness.

"I'm not going to push you into the Gorge. That wouldn't be right. No, I'll just leave you here with no way out except one. It's up to you when you take it. When you're desperate enough, you'll step into the darkness. You'll know what I know."

He stepped off. The emptiness seeped over him. His grinning face was the last thing to be swallowed.

"When you're ready..."

CHAPTER SIXTEEN

If you find yourself trapped on a small slab of rock floating in an eternally hungry void, I recommend bringing along some playing cards. Maybe video games are more fun or something to watch movies on. Books, if you're into that sort of thing, though if you're going the analogue route there's only so many you can carry.

But a solid deck of playing cards is portable and there are tons of variation on solitaire. I didn't know any of them, but I also didn't have any playing cards. It was all academic, but if I ever got out of here I'd buy a pack of cards and be ready.

That plan didn't help me right now, but thinking about it did kill a few minutes.

Outside this emptiness, time was easy to ignore. There was always something to distract you, to help drown out the ticking of the big clock. But here, time wrapped around me and held tight. Its claustrophobic grip was like the ocean around a submarine held together by my will to resist. No matter how well-made the submarine, the ocean always won in the end.

I already felt the cracks at the edges of my sanity. Eternity was a long time, and I imagined that the universe had come and gone while I was here. Everything devoured. Everything but me and this bit of the Garden. And when I couldn't take it anymore, I'd step into the emptiness, and that would be that. Everything just gone.

It would have been nice to see Irene one more time before that. To say good-bye.

A massive shape, invisible but detectable like a shadow passing through a shadow, swam past me. The Dragon. Still out there. Still angry. Always.

It was a rotten deal. All I wanted was a door that led me back home, a girlfriend who cared enough to yell at me, and enough time to figure ourselves out. Now all I had was time.

The longer I sat there, the madder I got. Anger was a luxury guys like me couldn't afford. The world was always ready to step on us if we got out of line, but there was no world anymore.

I picked up one of the three rocks on this little island, and with a defiant shout, hurled it over the edge. It disintegrated in the void, sending out little ripples. Two immense eyes, burning red, opened. Maybe a thousand miles away. Maybe right next to me. The Dragon's ragged breath put a tremble in the island.

"Yeah, fuck you, too," I spat through clenched teeth. The sentence was indecipherable, but the sentiment was clear enough.

The Dragon's footsteps thundered as the edges of its great horned head shimmered in the emptiness. It snorted, and the heat almost knocked me off my feet.

I grabbed the second rock, bigger than the first. Big enough to smash someone's head in if you put enough weight behind it. I hurled the stone at the Dragon's face as the beast bellowed its rage.

The rock landed with a thud at my feet. Another reminder of my helplessness. It was all so futile. Something broke in me the way that something had broken in Monty. A leak sprung as my sanity took on water. The Dragon quieted. In the emptiness, someone laughed at me.

It was me.

It was kind of funny. Not ha-ha funny. These were incomprehensible forces, and the best I could do was throw a rock at them. If that didn't summarize my life, what did? Except in real life, I'd never thrown the rock. In real life, I'd always blinked when staring the metaphorical dragon in the face.

"Better late than never," I said. I didn't know what I meant by that, but it triggered a deep belly laugh. The kind I hadn't had in a long time. I sat on the fallen tree, and I laughed until it hurt. The Dragon studied me, and in its eyes, I saw galaxies.

I wiped my tears, catching my breath. "You'd have to be a little mote of matter to get it."

The Dragon closed its massive jaws as it stared at me. Not with malice. Something else. Curiosity. Understanding. No way I could know. No way to know if it even had a mind I could relate to in the first place, but I wouldn't lay odds on it.

Still, it didn't seem like it hated me right now.

"Don't suppose you'd let me out of here?" I asked.

It faded away as it lumbered deeper into the emptiness of its home.

"Thanks, anyway, big guy."

The Dragon was still out there, but the Gorge felt less hostile. It still didn't like me, but I was used to that. Lots of people didn't like me. I didn't expect the universe would have a higher opinion. I could live with it. What choice did I have?

The void was lighter now. Oppressive in a less personal way. In the quiet, I could think better.

If I had a door, I could escape. Anything could be a door. I took stock of what I had. A fallen tree. Some rocks. Some dirt. Not great door material.

I knelt down and scraped out a rectangular outline in the ground. The rock was not the ideal tool. It dug into my hands. I placed the smallest rock where a handle would be. The end result was more a symbolic representation of a door than a door itself, but there were no hard and fast rules. Just metaphysical guidelines.

"Please. Please, let this work. I just want to go home. Destroy the world. I don't care. I just want to see Irene one last time."

I didn't know who I was talking to. The Gorge. The Dragon. The sword. God, cackling madly in his tiny little prison. Whoever the hell might be listening.

I grabbed the rock, imagining it as a doorknob, and turned.

Something clicked.

Or I only imagined something clicked.

I pulled. The rock resisting, holding to the earth. I heard a creak. Like hinges.

Then the rock came loose. The door thudded shut. Loud. I heard it that time. No imagining.

In the emptiness, the Dragon watched. I couldn't see it, but it was out there.

I dropped to my knees and carved the outline deeper. The rock was a bad tool, but I carved until my hands were raw, until my breath grew ragged and my heart pounded in my chest. This would work. It had to work.

I dropped the rock back into a proper doorknob's place. I turned and pulled. The door of earth moved. Only an inch. But it moved. I put my back into it, straining until I had nothing else to give. Then I gave more. It never got farther than that inch.

Exhausted, I rolled on my back. It wouldn't open. Too many things working against me. The door was made of stone. It needed to be lifted open. I wasn't strong enough. And the Gorge didn't let its prisoners go. The Dragon might not have hated me, but it wasn't planning on doing me any favors.

"Okay. Okay." I stared off into the hungry emptiness. "Fuck me for trying. You win."

But at least I had tried. I gave myself some credit for that, and I hoped the universe would, too.

I walked to the edge. This was what Monty had meant when he said *when*, not *if*. There was only one way out. I took out my pack of cigarettes, tucked one in my mouth. It'd be nice to have a lighter. Another thing I'd have to remember to plan ahead for. Life lessons.

The door opened behind me with a creak and a heavy clonk.

"Goddamn it, Ortiz," said Irene. "Are those my cigarettes?"

CHAPTER SEVENTEEN

The Gorge shook with rage as my island of stone crumbled away. I dove through the door Irene had opened. Gravity went weird as the world went from horizontal to vertical. I landed hard, banging my elbow and chin. Maybe loosened a tooth, but I'd made it.

The Dragon's hot, ragged breath poured through the darkened doorway. I jumped to my feet and slammed the door shut. I put my ear to it, heard rumbling.

Irene said, "What the hell, Ortiz?"

I put my finger to my lips as I checked the windows. Things looked okay. I was back in my shitty little apartment, which was a trap of its own, but if I had to pick my poison . . .

I'd made it. I'd escaped the Gorge without losing my mind.

I definitely had. This wasn't all a hallucination of my broken sanity.

It had to be real.

But what was real?

Monty had said something about the Dragon having its claws in him forever.

"How long was I gone?" I asked.

"Like two days," said Irene.

"That's all?"

She said, "Maybe three."

I took her by the shoulders. "Was it two or three?"

"Damn it, Jay." She recoiled. "What's wrong with your eyes?"

"Two or three?" I repeated.

She looked away. "I don't know. Hard to keep track of time here."

I laughed. She had no idea.

"Ortiz, if you've gone crazy on me..." She pulled out of my grip. "And what the hell happened to your eyes?"

I went to the bathroom. The blazing inferno was gone. Red eyes stared back at me in the mirror. Not bloodshot. Not irritated. A deep, bright crimson, like the Dragon's eyes. Like Monty's. The longer I gazed into them, the deeper they became. There was no bottom. Only an irradiated glow left over from the birth of the universe, background radiation of the big bang. And something else even more ancient and incomprehensible.

I splashed my face with water, dabbed myself with a dirty towel. It didn't fix the problem, but it wasn't really a problem. It was inevitable.

Maybe I had lost it, and this was all a hallucination. I'd blink, and I'd be back there. I sat down on my couch and shut my eyes. Couldn't blink if I never opened them again.

Irene said, "Hey, are you okay?"

Her fingers glided gently across the back of my hand. A desperate mind might fool itself into believing she was actually there.

"Is this real?" I asked.

"What kind of question is that?"

"I guess you wouldn't admit it if it weren't."

"Don't think this act will keep me from being pissed at you."

Her voice had that strange combination of irritation and concern. It sounded so much like her. Maybe too much like her. Like I imagined she'd sound if she were here.

I could picture her. She'd be glaring, but then she'd see my trauma, and it would make her uncomfortable, edgy. She didn't know what to do with vulnerability. Not mine. Not her own.

"Can you at least give me my cigarettes?" she grumbled.

Eyes shut tight, I smiled as I handed her the pack.

That was Irene, all right. As she was. As I imagined her.

In the end, that was what we all did. We only built simulated versions of the world around us and the people in it. The Dreaming World, the Waking World. I finally got why the Dreaming one was the real one. It was all a shared hallucination.

Smoke went up my nostrils, and I coughed, opening my eyes.

Irene took another drag on her cigarette. "Where the hell did you even go?"

I rubbed my blurry vision.

"I went for cigarettes for you, and then . . . it doesn't matter. Not right now."

She glared. Exactly like I'd imagined. Exactly like she would. It put a smile on my face. If my mind had been broken and this was all a fragile illusion, then it was close enough. I wouldn't poke at it.

Monty had stared oblivion in the eyes, and he'd screamed. But not me. I'd go mad quietly. No big deal. The same way I did everything.

It had taken more than a door to get me out of the Gorge. It took someone caring enough to try.

"You came for me."

"Damn right," she said. "You're nuts if you think I'm letting you leave me here alone."

"I love you," I said.

She puffed on her cigarette, letting the smoke billow without even inhaling it. "Yeah, that's cool."

It might not have been love that helped open that door, but it didn't matter. Love was just a label. In the whole universe, there was nobody else who would've come for me.

I smiled at Irene, but she looked away.

"Your eyes are creepy as hell," she said. "You know that, right?"

"You'll get used to it," I said.

That got a smile out of her.

"The bathroom isn't on fire anymore?" she asked.

I opened the front door and windows. The fiery version of the world didn't appear.

"What's that mean?" she said.

"I don't know. Something changed."

"It'd be nice to have some real answers for once."

"Okay." I took her hand. "The burning world was a message from the universe. By giving Horace the sword, I'd placed the world in jeopardy."

"And why did it change again?"

"Because I'm going to get the sword back."

"So your eyes get weird and now you're ready to take charge?" she asked.

"The eyes are just a side effect. I went into the darkness, and I came out alive. If I can handle that—if I'm not just insane right now and imagining all this while clawing my eyes out in the endless emptiness—then I can handle Horace."

Irene appraised me, and for the first time ever, she liked what she saw without reservation.

"Maybe you can," she said.

"We can," I said. "I'll talk to the sword. You talk to Horace. With some luck, we might be able to get him to give it up."

"Last time you wanted to do it alone."

"And look how that worked out."

She said, "Yeah, but I think maybe you were right. He hates me."

"He doesn't hate you."

"Are you stupid? All Horace and I do is antagonize each other."

"Sure, but you're not dead."

"That's a pretty low bar for love."

I chuckled. "I didn't say he loved you, and you do irritate the crap out of him. But there's something there. Something that keeps him from having you killed."

"What? For irritating him?"

"He's had people killed for less. And you really, really irritate him."

She smiled malignantly, but the smile dropped. "Maybe me going isn't such a great idea, then. If I irritate him while he has that sword it'll only make things worse."

"So don't irritate him."

Expecting her and Horace to be in the same room and not work each other's nerves was like expecting a shark and a tiger to be friendly. Provided you could get a pool shallow enough for the tiger but deep enough for the shark. Although they might not bother each other. Different ecosystems and all that.

Irene snapped her fingers, and I abandoned the metaphor.

"We'll worry about that when we need to," I said.

We exited the apartment through the door that lead back to the Waking World. Nothing peculiar happened.

"Maybe you should buy some sunglasses," she said.

"Normal people won't notice," I replied.

"I meant for me."

We got in the car.

"This doesn't seem like a plan," she said.

"We drive to Horace's place. We get him to give the sword to us," I said. "How hard can it be?"

"Well, when you put it like that."

I leaned over and kissed her. "Maybe just don't talk right away."

CHAPTER EIGHTEEN

None of Horace's crew tried to stop us. Instead, they quite helpfully opened the doors and led us into his study. He stood at the bay windows that overlooked the estate. A funny thing to see because Horace never opened the curtains. Too afraid someone might take a shot at him. Now he didn't give a damn because the sword protected him. I didn't see it, but I felt its power reflected off him. It was somewhere nearby.

Irene said, "Hiya, Horace."

"Didn't expect to see you again," said Horace. "Or you." He pointed to my eyes. "Looks good on you."

"Horace," I said, "you have to give me back the sword."

He chuckled. "I don't have to do shit. I thought we already established that. You gave me the sword. Now I'm going to use it to take what's mine."

He reached into his jacket and pulled out an automatic pistol. I felt the connection. The boon had changed shape. A sword was a little old-fashioned.

"It won't make you happy," I said.

Horace shook his head. "What the hell are you talking about? Who's happy? Happy is just a word suckers use to convince them their shitty lives aren't shitty."

"Not the happy speech again," said Irene.

Horace smirked, tucked the gun back into his jacket. "Nobody asked you to come back and bother me."

"What would Mom think if she saw you now?" asked Irene.

He snarled. "You think your mom was some angel? She always

knew what I did to get my money. She kept out of it, but she wasn't stupid."

"You were always an asshole, Horace," said Irene. "But now you're a godawful piece of shit."

They locked eyes. There was a lot of hate between these two. I'd underestimated just how much, which was saying something.

"That sword . . . gun destroys everyone who uses it eventually," I said. "Always."

Horace laughed. "You don't think I know that? Jeez, Ortiz, no wonder you were always such a loser."

He sat at his desk. "Okay. So let's say I give you back this gun. What happens next?"

"Everybody walks away alive," I said.

"That's the best you've got? Like I need to be safe. Everything I have I got by beating some other schmuck to death for it. You think this house, this suit, these fucking morons"—he gestured to the goons in the room—"are here because I waited politely for the world to give them to me? Because I played nice?"

"The schmuck speech," said Irene.

"Damn right, it's the goddamn schmuck speech. It's how the world works. If you'd ever listened to me—really listened, instead of being such a spoiled little shit—you'd know that. But no, you always had to be yapping and whining. Didn't stop you from living under my roof, did it? All that food you ate, those fancy schools I paid for, they were paid for with blood. And you knew that the whole time. Now you're acting self-righteous about it. Give me a fucking break."

"I was just a kid."

"You *were* just a kid. Now you're a grown-ass woman, still under my roof, eating my food." He glared at me. "Sleeping with this damn idiot."

Irene's face pinched in rage. I thought she might dive across the desk and try to brain him with her staff.

"Fuck you, Horace." She spun and walked out of the room.

"Yeah, fuck you, too," he grunted. "Hey, I got her to shut up. I'm telling you, this gun is the best thing that ever happened to me. No offense on that idiot remark, Ortiz. I never thought you were stupid. Just gutless."

"Thanks."

He nodded. "Guys like you always think guys like me are stupid.

I know I'm going to die ugly. I've always known. Hell, maybe one of these idiots will shoot me in the back." He pointed to the closest muscle. "Maybe you."

The muscle said, "No, sir. Not me."

Horace grinned. "Of course, you'd say that."

He leaned over his big, big desk.

"I know how the world works. The gun gives me an edge, but everybody pays the piper eventually. I'm going to get everything due to me before I have to pay it."

"And if you destroy the world in the process?" I asked, already knowing the answer.

"Fuck the world. What's the world ever done for me?"

Horace smirked. He wasn't indifferent to the danger he posed. He relished it. How much of that was Horace and how much of that was the gun was anyone's guess. They were one and the same now. I'd picked the right guy to unlock all the potential of the gun. And the wrong guy. The absolute worst guy.

The gun brought out the worst in him, but he brought out the worst in it in return. The gun wanted to be used, but it radiated anger, now. Hate. A boundless rage that would consume the world, just like Monty wanted.

Horace set the gun on the desk. I could make a move for it. If I got it in my hands then it would be mine again. I knew that much. He leaned back in his chair, put his hands behind his head, his feet on the desk. His playful grin dared me to try.

I wasn't afraid or reluctant. If I made a grab and failed, so what? The gun didn't want to hurt me. It hated everything. Everything but me. From me, it wanted something else. Approval, maybe? Like a naughty puppy eager to make me happy; but also, out of the cage and all too happy to chew up the couch and piss on the carpet. I'd be mad, but it was a puppy. It couldn't think that far ahead.

While I was communing with the gun, I missed my chance.

Sighing, Horace picked up the gun. "What'd I tell you? Gutless."

I almost felt sorry for him. He'd always seen the world in terms of power, but he didn't see this.

I said, "This isn't going to play out the way you think."

"Get the hell out of my house, and take my ungrateful daughter with you."

I stared Horace right in his sneering face, and my burning red eyes caused him to blink. The room chilled. A couple of Horace's goons shifted uncomfortably at the sight of their boss being openly challenged. Standing up to Horace was a good way to end up with a couple of busted knees.

His eyes narrowed. His face tightened.

I said, "I learned something from you a long time ago. When someone has power, they don't waste time talking. They don't make threats. They don't ask. They just do what they want."

I moved closer.

"Make me leave."

Horace nodded to one of his guys. "Shoot this asshole, wouldja?"

"I wouldn't," I said.

The muscle in a blue blazer pulled his own gun and pointed it at me. Before he could pull the trigger a weather vane crashed through the window behind him. It buried itself in his back with enough force to drive itself through his body and end up sticking into the floor. He gurgled in surprise at a pinned forty-five-degree angle as his blood pooled on the ground. He tried talking, but couldn't. Collapsed lung, probably.

I'd never seen the weather vane before, but it was an impressive wrought iron design with a giant chicken topper. How it ended up here, coming through that window at that particular moment, was a mystery. The universe had a playful side.

Horace pointed to another guy. "You."

"That's a bad idea," I said.

The second goon drew his gun and aimed. He hesitated to pull the trigger.

I said, "You don't have to—"

The gun blew up in his hand. I'd seen a gun do that once. An old one. The barrel split. Ruined the gun, but no serious damage to the shooter. But a piece of shrapnel came off this one, struck him in the eye. Must have been at just the right angle to drive it deep into his brain. He stumbled for a moment, tried to steady himself with a hand on nothing, and collapsed. Like the weather vane guy, he wasn't quite dead, but he was on his way.

"Damn it." Horace aimed his gun—my gun—at me. "Gotta do everything myself."

His hostility washed over me. His and the gun's. It was almost enough to get the job done. Almost. But he only pointed it at me. His hands trembled. Sweat beaded on his face.

"What's the problem?" I asked. "Maybe it's because we both know it's not your gun."

His jaw clenched. He found the will to pull the trigger. The gun clicked. It wanted to be used, but I was the bearer. I was in charge. He squeezed over and over again, the steady click of the hammer highlighting his impotence.

I reached across the desk, put my hand on the gun. It stuck to his sweaty palms, clinging as much to him as he to it.

"You said it was mine," wheezed Horace. "You said I could keep it."

I never said any such thing, but he wasn't talking to me. Someone moved in the corner of my eye. I mistook it for one of Horace's goons. No threat there. My mistake.

Monty's golden hand touched my arm, burning away the flesh. There was pain, but it was a distant thing, like the nerves themselves were destroyed, leaving no sensation, not even numbness. Just the stench of smoke and rot.

"Well, hello." Grinning, Monty pulled me away from Horace before releasing me. "Now how in the world did you get out of the Gorge so quickly?"

"Just lucky, I guess." His blackened handprint, complete with fingerprints, had withered everything from the forearm down. "You're working with Horace?"

"Surprised?"

"He's using you, Horace," I said.

Horace said, "If he lets me keep the gun, then I don't care."

"*Now* you're okay with being under somebody else's thumb?"

Frowning, he tucked the gun back in his coat. "Just kill him already. I'm sick of listening to him."

Monty's body of light burned brighter. "I thought when I left you in the Gorge that you'd be in there for a few decades at least, that you'd see the truth. But you're here now. You're different. But still you keep insisting on trying to stop me."

"You don't know what will happen if you kill me," I said. "We're linked."

"Maybe we'll both die," he said. "I could live with that, so to speak."

He lunged at me. I grabbed one arm, but his other hand caught me by the throat. Both my palm and my neck sizzled against his touch. The pain was brief and distant. I felt myself dying as my cells dried up, one by one. His hold was unbreakable. I sank to my knees as it all began to slip away.

Irene stepped up from nowhere and smashed Monty across the back of the head with her staff. An unnatural amount of force sent him flying across the room. He went through the wall, leaving a Monty-shaped hole seared in it like a cartoon character.

She took my hand and helped me up. "Are you okay?"

"I don't know." I cradled my damaged arm. I could still feel myself dying. It had slowed, but it wasn't stopping.

She delicately touched my neck. There wasn't any pain. No nerves to feel it. My head felt heavy, like my neck might snap if I turned it too quickly.

"We need to get you to a hospital," she said.

"It won't help," I said.

Irene ran her fingers along her staff. It had a few cracks in it now.

The wall disintegrated as Monty walked through.

She tightened her grip. "I'll shove this up your ass if you take another step."

Monty rubbed his head. Sparks drifted upward. "That's not what the staff is for. What would Leo say if he could see you now, taking his venerated boon of wisdom and threatening to hurt someone with it? Try something like that again, and it will surely break."

Irene didn't back down. "Ortiz, get the gun. I'll handle this guy."

"Yes, Ortiz," said Monty. "Do get the gun. If you can."

The connection between me and the gun had been weakened. Horace still couldn't use it against me, but now that Monty was here, it was two against one. The balance of power was too much. Plus, there was that whole dying slowly thing.

"I can't," I said.

Monty said, "I'm going to kill you both now, and you should both know it's all been for nothing. Nothing you've done matters or changes anything. But soon, you won't have to worry about that at all."

He moved toward us, but a beam of heavenly light sliced through the ceiling, cutting a spotlight between us. Viv materialized in a vision of light, like a magical hologram.

"Is this the way you want things?" she asked.

"Still hiding away, Viv. Still afraid?"

"I'm not a fool. Still, I can't let you kill him."

"I'm curious how you plan on stopping me."

Her gleaming sword plummeted through the hole in the ceiling to drive itself blade-first before her. Her voice boomed from everywhere. "Take up my boon and prove yourself worthy!"

Every thug in the place made a play for the sword. They punched and clawed their way through each other in a mad scramble.

"What the hell is this?" asked Horace.

Before Monty could answer, one of the goons grabbed the sword and raised it over his head. A golden light enveloped him, and the others all stepped away, their heads bowed.

"Arise, my champion!" bellowed Viv.

The goon smiled as he was filled with the power of truth and justice. It emanated off him in waves, and he physically changed, becoming twenty-five percent handsomer. His teeth gleamed, and damned if there wasn't a sparkle in his eye. I knew then that everything would be all right.

Horace shot the champion in the head. The gun practically vaporized his skull, sending some blood and brains splattering on the nearby goons. His corpse fell over, but the sword jumped out of his hand, drove itself back into the floor.

"Take up my boon and prove yourself worthy!" shouted Viv again.

Despite what had happened to the previous champion, the thugs all fought for it with even more fervor this time. One guy bit another one right on the face.

"Arise, my champion!"

Horace took a shot, but the new champion was ready. He deflected the bullet with his sword. The champion moved forward, blocking each shot fired by Horace like a Jedi Knight. He used one hand to toss the desk aside like it was made of balsa wood and seized Horace by the collar.

"For your wickedness, you shall now perish."

Monty put a hand on the champion's shoulder, and with a stifled scream he dissolved into a smoldering skeleton. The sword tumbled back to the middle of the room, driving itself into the floor.

"Take up my boon and prove yourself worthy!"

The few surviving guys left all resumed fighting for it.

Viv said, "You need to leave before I run out of champions." She vanished in another flash of light.

We ran out of the room as the next in line claimed the sword. Amid the echo of gunshots, a bullet whizzed a couple of inches past my ear.

Irene led us to the backyard. The Boatman and his boat sat in the swimming pool.

"I'd get on while you can," he said.

"I haven't got the gun back," I said.

Irene climbed in the boat. "You can't. You're still not ready yet."

"How do you know that?"

She shook the staff at me. "I'm your guide, remember?"

She pulled me aboard, and the boat sailed into the deep end of the pool as mists enveloped us.

Monty stepped on the patio. His body was living flame, white hot and enraged. He stopped at the pool's edge.

"She can't hide forever," he said.

"She knows," said the Boatman as we drifted deeper into the misty waters.

CHAPTER NINETEEN

Things lurked in the encircling mists. They moved about just out of sight, though once I thought I saw a scarred, vaguely human face. Only for a moment.

"For your own safety keep your hands in the boat at all times," said the Boatman.

The mist curled over the boat's prow. It swallowed the Boatman and crept in a tight circle around Irene and me. I expected it to consume us. In our place, a couple of corpses sailing on a boat toward a destination never to be reached.

I squeezed Irene's hand. "I'm sorry I got you into this."

"It's a little late for apologies."

"In my defense, I told you not to take the staff," I said.

Fingertips of fog wrapped around her staff. She brushed them away. "Oh, so now you're blaming me."

"I'm not blaming anyone. I didn't exactly pick the sword, either."

"No, you don't ever pick anything." She pulled away from me. The fog slipped around her, threatening to pull her into its cold embrace. "Things are picked for you."

"I picked you."

"Like hell, you did. I picked you because I'm a fucking idiot."

The fog pressed down on me like a weight. The mists were bringing out the worst in us, tapping into everything that made us a rotten couple. Every tiny flaw, every massive deficit. Ours was a fragile, screwed-up love. One push in the wrong direction on the wrong day, and we'd hate each other.

But not if I could help it.

Before I could offer another apology, she mumbled, "How are you feeling?"

The fog rolled away, taking the hostility with it. Or maybe the words pushed away the fog. Like most of this crap the distinction was blurry.

My arm was in bad shape. Withered and gangrenous. It didn't hurt, but that somehow made it worse. Like a stiff breeze might break it off, drifting into a swirl of ashes like a dandelion. My neck must have been pretty awful, but thankfully, I couldn't see that.

"It's not as bad as it looks."

"It better not be. They probably have something in Avalon to fix it." There was a slight tremor in her voice. It was more hope than truth. She was worried. Hell, I was worried.

"I'm sorry, too," I said. "For everything."

"That's a lot to be sorry for."

"Just trying to be thorough."

We shared a chuckle. The fog melted away, and the sun illuminated Gwen standing on the shores of Avalon.

"Everybody out," said the Boatman.

We eagerly climbed out onto the beach.

"That was different than last time," she said.

"Every journey has its own hazards." He pushed away. "Good luck. You'll need it."

Pain hit me suddenly. Hard enough to buckle my knees. I collapsed in writhing agony.

Irene cradled me. "What's happening?"

"The power of Avalon is healing him," said Gwen. "Guess it started with the nerves first."

It took about an unpleasant minute while the magic restored me. The damage disappeared without a trace, and after, even the memory was gone.

"What happens when I leave Avalon again?" I asked.

"Answer unclear." Gwen shrugged. "Try again later. You blew it."

"Monty interfered," said Irene.

"Of course, he interfered. What did you expect?"

She led us through the forest. This time, the forest seemed less hostile, but also, less magical. Maybe it was like the trip with the Boatman. Each journey was its own. But, no, I knew it was something else. Avalon felt wrong in some small way. I couldn't quite put a name on it, though.

Viv was waiting for us in the throne room.

"Thanks for saving us," I said.

"I couldn't just let you die," she replied. "You and your claim to the sword might be the only thing keeping Monty in check."

"Or he could have killed me, and he'd die with me, and you'd be free of this problem."

Viv half-smiled. "I had considered it, but since we don't really know the answer, I didn't want to take the chance."

"So what do we do now?" asked Irene.

"Nothing," said Viv. "There is nothing to do. You two stay here as my guests. Monty can't come here. You'll be safe. Avalon provides. Plenty of room. We won't even have to see each other."

"You're letting Horace keep the sword, and Monty do whatever he wants while you hide away in this magical shelter?" Irene glared at the bearers. "Aren't you supposed to be paragons, bearers of great responsibility?"

Gwen looked away, but Viv locked stares.

"Sometimes, prudence is the most responsible choice."

Irene didn't break eye contact. "You're fucking cowards. Sugarcoat it any way you want, but you're giving up."

Viv blinked. Just once. It was like getting the sun to blink.

"Do you have any better ideas?"

What I said next surprised me, because Irene was right. Viv's plan was giving up, and I was great at giving up. It was second nature, even if it didn't always work out.

But I couldn't stomach this. In another universe, Roger had beaten me to the sword, and none of this was my problem. In another world, I wouldn't be indirectly responsible for the deaths of eight or nine people, some of them genuinely good. I'd lost count. In another world, I was lying in a shallow grave, forgotten by everyone.

But not this world.

"I need to sit in the Siege."

"How do you know about the Siege?" asked Gwen.

"Monty says you hid it in Avalon," I replied.

Viv folded her arms and took measure of me. "He's wrong. I didn't hide it. It hid itself."

"So it's here?" I asked.

"What's this Siege?" said Irene.

"It doesn't matter," said Viv. "It's lost to the ages. It hasn't been seen in centuries."

"I've seen it," I said.

"In other circumstances, I'd call you a liar. But these are strange times." Viv stood and walked from the room. We knew enough to follow without being asked.

"Where are we going?" I asked.

Viv took a random turn down a hall of doors. "You tell me, Ortiz."

I approached the first door and opened it without hesitation. The familiar lonely little chair sat in its lonely little room.

Viv gestured for me to step through first. "You remain an unending wellspring of surprises."

Viv spoke with hushed reverence. "Behold, the Siege Perilous."

Gwen glared at the chair like it had run over her favorite puppy. "Not this damned thing. I thought it was lost centuries ago."

"Avalon is where the lost things go," said Viv.

"It's been following me," I said.

Viv smiled. "What more proof do we need? You must sit in it."

Irene said, "Ortiz, you cannot sit in that thing."

"He must sit," said Viv.

"He'll die," said Gwen.

"No one dies in Avalon," said Viv.

"Why don't you sit in it, then?"

Viv said, "It didn't appear to me."

Gwen said, "Isn't that convenient? Ortiz, that chair might not kill you, but I guarantee it'll fuck you up."

"Or he'll pass its test," said Viv. "He's already done what couldn't be done."

Irene asked, "Isn't the Siege Perilous for the knight destined to find the Grail? Are we looking for that?"

"We already have the Grail." Gwen reached behind her back and produced her cup like a cartoon character.

A light came into Irene's eyes. "You're Gwynevere."

Gwen shrugged. "Don't make a thing about it."

"But Gwynevere never had the Grail."

"The stories get a lot of things wrong."

"The Siege is an ancient test. Older than the cup," said Viv. "A test of worthiness."

"You and your stupid tests of worthiness," said Gwen.

Irene pushed herself between me and Viv. "Ortiz isn't worthy. We all know that."

Viv waved her off. "And yet, the Siege appeared to him."

While they argued, I studied the chair. The cup and the staff radiated a quiet power, a subtle vibration in the air. The Siege was different. Its aura was subtler. It was a small tingle in my fingers and toes, down my spine. The arms beckoned me to brave its challenge. Its glowing runes offered secrets. Its legs threatened to trample me to death.

The Siege was full of promises, wonderful, terrible, both at once, and it kept placing those promises before me. It didn't actually care if I took up the offer. Didn't like me much at all. It was odd to register disdain from a piece of furniture, but that was the world I lived in now.

"I'll sit in it."

They all turned their heads toward me as if they'd just remembered I was still in the room.

Irene said, "Ortiz, you can't—"

"What happens if I pass?"

"I don't know," said Viv.

"What happened to the Grail guy?"

"Perceval," said Irene.

"Yeah. Him. What happened to him?"

"Nothing," said Gwen.

"Thus proving his worthiness." Viv stood over me. She seemed a few inches taller than before. Her expression remained unreadable. "The act of sitting—of choosing to sit—is transformative."

"What does that even mean?" said Irene.

"Metaphysical guidelines," I said.

Viv smiled. "You understand, then."

"No," I said. "Not really."

Viv's smile widened as she put her hand on my chest. Unlike the first time she'd touched me, I felt light and reassured. "The Siege's return means something. The longer the gun stays in the hands of your champion—"

"Horace is not Ortiz's champion," said Irene.

"Didn't Ortiz choose him?"

That hit me hard in the gut. I had chosen him. I'd given cosmic power to a real piece of shit, and I'd known he was a piece of shit when I gave it to him, so I couldn't play innocent.

"Isn't Monty the real problem anyway?" asked Irene.

"It's all connected," said Viv. "The sword, the Dragon, the Gorge, Monty, Ortiz. If Ortiz reclaims the sword then perhaps it can all be fixed."

"I almost had it," I said. "If not for Monty."

"Yeah, and he almost killed you," said Irene. "That already proves that you're not worthy."

"One failure doesn't equal eternal failure," said Viv.

"Yes, but Ortiz is great at failure. It's the only thing he is great at."

Gwen said, "You can't force him. That's not how the chair works."

"No, I can't," said Viv. "It's his choice to make, though he's the one who brought it up in the first place."

I studied the chair. Its disdain gave way to acceptance. It didn't want me to sit in it, but it didn't have a choice. Larger forces had drawn us together against our will. They couldn't make me sit, but if I chose to sit, the Siege didn't get a vote.

Irene grabbed my arm. "You're nuts if you think I'm just going to stand here and watch you kill yourself."

I said, "What if the sword found me for a reason? What if it all led up to this?"

Gwen said, "Viv, you've been around forever. Tell him that there's no such thing as destiny."

"I can't tell him that because I don't know." Viv walked around the chair, caressing it. "None of us in this room know what the universe wants. If it wants anything at all. Nor can we say that the Siege Perilous speaks for the universe. In the end, despite everything, it's only our choices that matter, even if they often matter in unexpected ways."

Irene said, "Don't tell me this New Age bullshit is working on you, Ortiz."

"It kind of is," I replied. "We're in Avalon. This is Gwynevere. You've got that staff. I had a sword that is made to kill a dragon. A magic chair that makes me better isn't that stupid. What else can I do? Stay here in Avalon forever while Monty and Horace make the world awful because of me?"

Scowling, she tightened her grip. "You're crazy if you do this."

She had that tone in her voice. She was looking for a fight, and in other circumstances, I might have taken the bait. She wanted me to waste time trying to convince her that this was right. The argument could've gone round and round for hours. Maybe forever.

I took her hand in mine, kissed her once. "I'll do what I have to do. You do what you have to do."

"You idiot." She stepped back, but she didn't leave the room.

I approached the chair. Its runes flared brighter, and I swear I heard it sigh.

I sat. Didn't hesitate. Perceval wouldn't have.

The room disappeared. An endless black expanse stretched all around me, and I thought I must have fallen back into the Gorge. In a panic, I tried to stand, but I was glued to the chair.

A small blue light appeared in the distance. It expanded slowly until I could make it out as a TV screen. It blared at me as it switched through channels from CNN to *Green Acres* reruns to Tom & Jerry cartoons. A bit of motion to my left caught my attention. A withered old hand held a remote, clicking it impatiently.

"Ms. Cuervo?" I asked.

She sat in her beat-up recliner beside me. She squinted at the TV. "I am the ineffable and irreversible judgment of the Siege Perilous. This is merely the form you've elected to give me." She sucked on her dentures. "That's not too complicated for you to understand, is it?"

"No."

Her wrinkled face puckered in a condescending smile. "Good. Let's get to it. I'm going to spare you the suspense. You are not worthy."

I shrugged. "Yeah, no, I already figured that, even before I sat."

She shook her head. "Yet you did it anyway."

I shrugged again. There wasn't a lot else I could do stuck in the chair. "I thought maybe confidence would count for something."

"Confidence is more often the mark of fools than heroes," she said. "And you weren't really confident. Just faking it."

She turned up the volume on the TV as an episode of *The Twilight Zone* started. Not the original show, but the first revival. Not that other one. Or that other one after that. The familiar theme washed over me as things stirred in the dark. I assumed them to be Ms. Cuervo's cats, or the astral simulation, but these were different. Their eyes were red, and when they strayed into the edge of the TV's light they were misshapen lumps of furry flesh.

I shouted over the TV. "If I'm not worthy then what am I doing here?"

Annoyed, she turned down the TV. Not all the way. Just enough that it would still make it difficult to concentrate on what she said.

"You're a scumbag and a screw-up. Foolish at best, stupid at worst. You've caused harm to many around you, just by existing, even before gaining your boon. And once you claimed it, you continued to make a series of bad decisions that only made things worse and have placed the whole world in jeopardy. But I thought you might want to make a case for yourself."

"Would it matter?"

"Ineffable and irreversible. But everyone's given a chance. It's in the rules. And don't ask who made those rules. Waste of everyone's time."

"The problem is that I don't disagree," I replied. "My only defense is that I never asked for the goddamn sword."

"That's not much of a defense," she said. "Greatness is not a burden requested, but a burden borne well."

"I've never wanted to be great."

"What we want is rarely what we get. But when that sword came to you, you didn't aspire to be better."

"Didn't think that was an option."

The TV filled with angry static. I closed my eyes from its blinding light.

Ms. Cuervo said, "It's always an option, dumbass."

"That's stupid," I said. "I'm not a great guy, but I'm not the worst. Nothing in my life prepared me for all this magical madness. I can't handle my own life, and the universe throws a magic sword at me and expects me to know what to do with it? That's not fair."

"And yet, without that sword, you'd be buried in an unmarked grave, mourned by none."

The TV snapped off. A soft light came from everywhere, and a simulation of Irene stood before me.

"Almost none." She leaned on her staff. "You should have listened to her."

"You're not her," I said.

Irene glared at me in an all too familiar way but said nothing.

"I could've done better," I said. "Is that what you want me to say? Because, yeah, I could have, but I think I've done okay for what I had to work with."

She remained silent, judging me.

"I'm not some mythical knight out of a fairy tale. Excuse me for being human."

The judgmental expression faded to something else. Pity. Contempt. A combination of the two. And maybe a touch of affection. If it wasn't Irene it was a hell of a simulation.

"Just kill me then," I grumbled. "I'm tired of this conversation."

Irene's face softened. She reached out, placed a hand under my chin. It wasn't her, and it was her. Out of all the people I'd let down, and it was a long list, I regretted her most of all.

She leaned close and whispered in my ear. "Nobody dies in Avalon."

If she said anything after that, I couldn't hear it over my own screaming as my body was consumed in fire.

CHAPTER TWENTY

I'd seen a guy burned to death once. Hazard of being on Horace's payroll. There was screaming and writhing and every horrifying other thing you'd imagine, but I mostly remembered the smell. Like hamburger left too long on the grill. Technically, the fire hadn't killed him. I'm sure it would have eventually, but once he'd suffered enough Little Jake had been disgusted enough to just shoot the poor bastard in the head. It'd been an ugly way to go, and afterward, I'd done some research into the process. Morbid curiosity.

It hurts like hell at first, but once the nerves are burnt, there's nothing to feel anymore.

Magic fire didn't burn nerves. The flames raged around me, not so much as blackening my socks, but devouring my soul. I'd always assumed my soul to be a withered, useless little thing, easily extinguished.

I'd been wrong, and I felt every goddamn second of it.

The pain became background noise, an angry static clawing at my body. Every so often, the agony lessened to merely excruciating and my senses would return. I was back in the room with Irene, Gwen, and Viv. I'd already screamed myself hoarse. As I gurgled, I caught snippets of conversation.

Viv said, "The Siege Perilous must do its work."

"It's fucking killing him!" said Irene.

"No one dies in Avalon."

"That makes it worse," said Irene.

I lost track of everything as a fresh layer of my innermost self burned away. The flames dug deeper. The chair poked and prodded the vital pieces of me. There was no malice. Just a deep curiosity at the idiot who had chosen to sit in it. The pain was merely a side effect.

"I'm getting him out of there." My vision cleared as Irene reached for me.

I spit out a strangled warning, shaking my head. If I'd been able, if my head wasn't killing me, if my unburning flesh wasn't boiling, I would have said that there was no escape. If Irene tried, the chair would just roast her, too.

"Don't," I croaked.

Irene scowled. "Fuck that."

Damn it, why wouldn't she ever listen to me? Just once.

"You must not interfere," said Viv.

The fire burned hotter. Tongues of white flame lashed out at Irene, forcing her back.

I ripped my right arm off the chair, like tearing off layers of skin and muscle. "Stay away. Please." I didn't actually say that, but whatever I grunted out, she got the message.

The Siege dragged my arm back onto the armrest as it pushed its way deeper. The soul was a complicated, many-layered thing. When I thought the last layer had been found, there was always another. One more unworthy piece of me. I'd never be worthy, but the chair wouldn't stop trying.

If I sat in this chair long enough, if the pain didn't drive me mad, if the wisp of a soul left at the end of the process was worth anything, I'd be a better man. More likely, I'd be a broken thing. Viv would shove whatever was left in one of Avalon's broom closets, and there, I'd spend eternity between a mop bucket and some rusty shields.

Irene wedged her staff between me and the chair.

"That is not what the staff is for," said Viv.

Irene worked the staff deeper and leaned her full weight against it. The Siege wouldn't give me up easily, but I peeled an inch or two. Enough that she could get deeper behind my back. The chair responded by turning up the heat, wrapping its fiery grip tighter.

She pushed harder with all the stubbornness she had. And it was a lot of stubbornness. A supernatural level of stubbornness. The kind of stubbornness that pulled me away from the Siege inch by inch. Her staff creaked audibly as cracks formed. It would break before she'd give up.

"Damn it, Ortiz," growled Irene. "Help me out here."

I pushed against the armrests. I managed to rise. Only half an inch. It took everything I had, but pain was a hell of a motivator.

Gwen took hold of the staff, adding her strength to the effort. Viv watched with an expression of mild curiosity.

The staff splintered and cracked. It wouldn't last much longer. Irene and Gwen screamed. I would have, but only a rasp came out of my throat. The staff broke in two as I was thrown to the floor.

The flames vanished. I curled up into a trembling, sweat-soaked ball. There was no obvious physical damage, but nothing seemed to be working.

Irene threw aside the pieces of the staff and knelt beside me. She turned my head toward hers. "Come on, baby. Stay with me." She wiped my face with her hands. It wasn't very effective, but it felt nice. "Tell me you're okay."

I gargled something unintelligible.

"You shouldn't have interfered," said Viv.

Gwen said, "He sat in your stupid chair. He didn't pass the test. He isn't worthy."

"You never understood," said Viv.

"None of us understand," said Gwen. "I was there. I saw Arthur's kingdom rise and fall. I saw the look on your face, Viv. You were as surprised as any of us."

Irene said, "Can you two hash out your problems later? Do you have a bedroom in this place? Someplace Ortiz could get some rest."

She tried getting me to my feet, but my legs were useless. Gwen braced me on the other side and helped. Viv, a frown on her smooth face, pushed them aside and hoisted me in her arms without the slightest effort. She carried me from the room, and the last thing I remember was seeing the Siege Perilous from over her shoulder. Just sitting there, waiting for the next sucker to come along.

Everything was a blur for a while. I slept a lot. Sometimes, I'd wake up, and in a haze, survey pieces of the room. The luxurious four-poster bed with silk curtains, soft bedding and too many pillows. Tapestries on the walls. Candelabras. All kinds of junk you'd see in a middle school girl's vision of a fairy tale bedroom.

There was also a chair. Every time I stirred, Irene would be there.

Sometimes, asleep herself. More often, awake. She'd take my hand and ask me how I was doing. I'd croak out how I was feeling better. She'd nod as if she didn't believe me but wanted to be supportive.

Eventually, my senses came back to me, and I could move again. Enough to get out of bed.

"You should be careful," she said.

"I'm fine." Sitting up, my head spun for a moment. "Mostly fine. How long has it been?"

"Hell if I know," she replied. "Time is weird here. Do you want something to eat?" She grabbed a silver tray laden with various meats and cheeses, but I pushed it away.

She pushed it back. "You need to eat."

I grabbed a piece of ham and shoved it down with a forced smile. That was enough for her.

"I told you not to sit in that damn chair," she said. "If I hadn't been there . . ."

"If you hadn't been there, the staff wouldn't have been broken," said Viv. Neither of us had seen her enter. Might have been magic. Might have been the way she moved silently.

"I don't give a damn about that staff," said Irene, picking up the broken pieces leaning against her chair.

Viv said, "By destroying the staff you have removed something vital from the world. There will be consequences."

"Screw consequences." Irene chucked a piece at Viv, who caught it in one hand.

"You stay in Avalon only by my good graces." Viv glided toward Irene and offered the half-staff back to her. "I'm eternal, but my patience isn't without limit."

Irene took back the staff. "People are more important than objects."

"Not these objects." Viv leaned closer to me, staring me in the face. "Do you feel any different now?"

"There's a tingle on my skin," I said. "Also, indigestion. But not in my stomach. More like in my soul, if that makes sense."

"Then perhaps there is still hope that the Siege Perilous did its work, despite your lover's interference."

Irene and I smiled at the word. Like kids hearing something naughty.

Without even saying good-bye, Viv flowed majestically from the room.

"Where's Gwen?" I asked.

"Saw her and Viv having a conversation. Couldn't hear it, but the body language was hostile on Gwen's part. Stormed away. Haven't seen her since."

"I'm surprised you're still carrying the staff pieces around."

"I'm not. They keep following me. Guess there's some magic left in the thing."

She knocked the two pieces together several times.

"So how do you feel?" I asked. "Any side effects from damaging it? You're linked, after all."

She shrugged. "I don't feel less wise, if that's what you're asking. And destroying a metaphysical representation of wisdom to save your dumb ass is on brand for our whole thing."

"Sorry about that."

Irene put down the pieces as she pushed me back onto the bed.

"Don't worry about it, lover."

She kissed me. An electric shock ran through my body. It wasn't a metaphor.

Irene jumped back with a yelp. "What the hell was that?"

I got to my feet. Energy coursed through me. I moved my hands through the air, trailing a spherical rainbow of lights. I felt Avalon all around me. Massive, ancient, alive with memories half-remembered and not quite forgotten.

The broken staff rattled and flew into my hands. I joined the halves, and the wood grew together. The healed staff blazed brightly for a moment before the power within me settled down.

"How did you do that?" asked Irene.

"I don't know."

I held the staff in a loose grip. It felt right in my hands. The staff whispered to me in a gentle, reassuring voice, but I wasn't its bearer.

I gave it back to Irene. Another electrifying zap passed through us. She took the staff back and smiled the sly grin of a person who knew more than you.

"I've got to show you something."

CHAPTER TWENTY-ONE

Irene led me through the halls of Avalon. I remembered how I felt following Leo. A bearer couldn't use their boon, but they would still be transformed by it. Did Irene knowing where to go qualify as using the staff? Or was she just wiser than she was ten minutes ago? It was a gray area. There were a lot of gray areas.

Whatever the answer, the transformation was too sudden. It was supposed to take place over decades as the boon exposed its bearer to powers. But here was Irene, walking with quiet purpose.

"Where are we going?" I asked.

Her ears were longer and pointed now. Like an elf. Or a fox. They twitched as she offered a sly smile, like she knew everything but didn't want to ruin it for me.

We walked into the bowels of the castle. This wasn't the kind of castle that should have had bowels, but I guess even enchanted realms needed storage space. The torches flickered, casting shadows on torn tapestries and discarded furniture pushed against the walls. There was an odor the further we went. Mold and dust and expired milk.

This was definitely not on the official Avalon tour, and we weren't supposed to be here. But I followed Irene, not bothering to ask any more questions. We'd get to the answers eventually. That much, I trusted.

We came to an old metal door, huge and formidable. It might have been rusted shut. Irene stamped her staff on the floor once, and it opened with a long, loud creaking. If Viv hadn't known we were down here, she would now.

Inside the room was a great big pile of junk. And another pile beside that. And another beside that. Piles upon piles of broken things. Shields and swords, chairs and tables, knickknacks and bric-a-brac. Some pieces more broken than others, but all of them in some state of decay.

"What is all this?"

"The slow death of Avalon," said Irene. "One piece at a time."

Viv cleared her throat behind us. "You don't belong here."

"Uh, sorry," I said.

Her face puckered. "How did you find this place?"

Her towering presence and accusatory tone was almost enough to make me sell out Irene. I stuck my hands in my pockets and looked at my feet.

"Just did."

"How long have you been hiding this?" asked Irene.

"It's none of your concern," said Viv. "And didn't you break the staff?"

"He fixed it," said Irene.

Viv focused her humorless gaze upon me. "How?"

I nudged a piece of broken vase with my shoe. "Just did."

"And he made it work better, too," said Irene. "Before, it was always like a little whisper in my head, but one I couldn't hear. Now it's clearer." Her ear bent toward the staff. "I still can't hear everything, but it says this room is important."

"This room, these things, don't matter," said Viv. "Avalon is eternal. Avalon endures."

I grabbed a chalice off a crooked table. Simply touching the table caused a leg to break off. It tipped over, spilling the rest of its contents. The chalice snapped in two in my hand. Avalon's endurance wasn't as endless as advertised.

"It's dying, isn't it?" I said. "It's that dragon in your basement, isn't it?"

Viv's face wasn't made for shock, but it was obvious. Irene's shock was easier to read.

"How did you figure that out?" asked Viv.

"What?" I replied. "I'm not an idiot."

She wasn't convinced.

"I'm not an idiot all the time," I said.

Viv, a tower in her black gown, slouched. She leaned against a chipped credenza that threatened to collapse under her weight.

"The dragon below us has slept since time began, but as Monty's madness infected his dragon, it gave Avalon's manifestation fitful dreams and nightmares. As it stirs, those nightmares threaten Avalon itself.

"It started small, with a crumbling bit of brickwork or a tear in a carpet. When I found such imperfections, I hid them away, pretended they weren't there. I trusted that Avalon would heal itself. But as it grew worse I knew that I only had one choice. If I couldn't kill the Dragon, then I could perhaps calm it by removing Monty from the equation.

"It worked at first. Avalon didn't heal, but it stopped dying. For a long time, it maintained its equilibrium. It was no longer perfect, but its imperfections were hidden. I hoped that was enough."

"But he got out again," I said, "and whatever happened in the Gorge made him crazier, more dangerous."

"You broke him," said Irene. "You broke the sword, the Dragon."

Viv straightened. Her eyes went cold. "I'm the bearer of my sword. I'm the keeper of Avalon, the most important bastion of magic, a cornerstone of reality itself. Was I to stand aside and let it die?"

"Don't act like you had noble motives. You hid here and left the Waking World to fend for itself. You were just protecting yourself and your home. You wrote off everything and everyone else a long time ago. You tried to talk us into doing the same."

"I won't stand by and be lectured—"

"The hell you won't."

Irene's ears flattened. Her voice took on that tone. The one I'd heard a hundred times before.

"You can act all high and mighty, but you're afraid. You were afraid of Monty before, and now that's he's come back, you're more afraid. You made everything worse, and now you don't know what to do. And you're hoping that someone else can clean up your mess. That's why you brought us here. That's why you had Ortiz sit in the Siege Perilous. And that's why you'll listen to me, because I carry the staff of guidance, and he's connected to the Dragon in a way you never will be."

Viv scowled. "Assuming I relent to your counsel, what do we do then?"

"I offer wisdom, not knowledge," said Irene. "I can't just tell you."

"Can't. Or won't?"

"Is there a difference?" I answered.

Irene jerked her thumb in my direction. "Look at him, understanding things."

I walked among the piles of junk. There was an answer here somewhere. Why else would I be here? Reality was messy, confusing, often pointless. But Irene carried the staff, and there had to be a reason she'd brought me here.

I grabbed a broken hand mirror with a tarnished silver frame. A spark jolted down my hand. The cracked glass repaired itself. Startled, I dropped it, and it shattered again.

Viv looked on with annoyance. It was only a broken thing in a room full of them, but I still felt guilty.

"Sorry." I knelt down and picked up the mirror again. I expected the jolt this time. The mirror's cracks mended. Its silver sparkled. I gently set the mirror down and picked up some shards of something. Bits jumped from the other piles and glued themselves together into a vase.

"The Siege Perilous has given you the power of restoration," said Viv.

"I guess I could fix all this stuff," I replied. "It might take a while, though."

"What would be the point other than to slow the death of Avalon? It's a stopgap, not a solution."

Irene, her ears twitching, that sly smile on her face, said nothing.

"I fixed the staff," I said. "Are there any other boons I could fix?"

Viv said, "You didn't simply fix it. You made it better."

"Right. So something made to fight a dragon might help. A lance or a shield or a holy hand grenade."

"Or a sword."

Viv's boon materialized in her hands. The shining blade gleamed with its own inner light.

"You said it was different than my sword," I said.

"It is," said Irene. "And it isn't."

"Except my sword is a gun now and in the hands of a psychopath."

"Which is why if I give you mine," Viv said, "you must promise to take better care of it."

"Bearers can't use boons."

"You are no ordinary bearer, Ortiz. You escaped the Gorge. You survived the Siege Perilous."

"I sort of cheated on both of those."

Lines creased Viv's face, and I saw that she was just as damaged as every bit of junk in this room. Not just metaphorically. She was Avalon, and all the flaws she'd hidden down here weren't only a product of the Dragon. All bearers were human, underneath all the other trappings they might pick up along the way. Viv was tired. The weight of hundreds, maybe thousands of years, bore down on her.

She was a fragile thing held together by willpower and failing magic.

"Will you die if I take it?" I asked.

"No one dies in Avalon."

It sounded a lot less like the truth surrounded by all this broken junk.

"I'm not worthy," I said.

"Who ever has been?"

She bowed, offered her sword to me. This must have been what King Arthur felt like. To be chosen. To have the universe point at you and say, "Don't fuck this up." All the while knowing that fucking it up was inevitable.

I reached for it, and the sword practically jumped into my hand. Another jolt nearly knocked me off my feet. The sword channeled all the magic of Avalon into me, and it was a lot of magic. A universe's worth of magic. The Siege Perilous had given me the power to do what no one else had ever done. With this sword in my hands—if I could contain everything it had to offer—I could do almost anything. This sword had made legends, but those legends had been the barest hint of what I could do. The beautiful agony threatened to tear my body apart. It was too much and not enough. Once you got a taste of it, power was a bottomless hunger.

Avalon quaked and crumbled around us. Fissures tore through the brickwork. The castle threatened to bury us, but it wouldn't matter. If I had the power, I could do anything.

I could do everything.

"Everything is more than anyone needs to do," said Irene.

Her words pulled me back to the world, though my senses still stretched out to ethereal planes. I glimpsed the invisible strands binding her to the staff. Delicate threads binding her body and soul to the boon.

The sword's tendrils burrowed deep into my own self, but a few loose patterns floated delicately across the room to Viv, collapsed on the floor.

I dropped the sword and checked on her. Turning her over was easy. Where before she'd been a bulwark, she was now a ghost, as if there were nothing in her gown. The wrinkles creasing her face threatened to swallow it whole. Her tiny eyes closed as a few more strands broke away. There were only a dozen left, dying embers only holding on because of Avalon's waning magic.

"I didn't mean to," I said. "I'll give it back."

She smiled at Irene, who smiled back. They both knew things I didn't, and while I was used to being the dumbest guy in the room, it sucked that even wielding the power of Avalon didn't change that.

Viv's hand fell to the sword at my side. Her sword, now bound to me.

She said, "Bear it well, Ortiz."

Her tiny, gray eyes closed.

CHAPTER TWENTY-TWO

We put Viv in one of the castle's many bedrooms and did our best to make her comfortable. She wasn't dead, but she didn't have much time left. Neither did Avalon. I hadn't taken all its magic, but the sword and the castle were tied together. All this magic stuff was.

"Tell me this will all work out," I said to Irene.

"It will all work out."

"Do you know that? Or are you just humoring me?"

She said, "You tell me."

"I'm getting kind of tired of this sagely wisdom crap."

"I'm not too keen on it myself, but here we are." She waved the staff in a circle, and it disappeared. "We should get going."

"Do you know the way out of here?" I asked.

She kissed me, and it felt like she meant it. No reservations. No second guesses.

"That, I know."

I followed her through the maze of a castle and the maze of a forest to the shores of Avalon. The Boatman was already waiting for us. His appearance had changed again. He wore a black hoodie that covered his face in shadows. Bony, pale hands stuck out of the sleeves. The boat was a hobbled-together raft taking on water.

"Is this an omen?" I asked.

His voice was dry and cracked. "Can't complain about the ride when you're taking most of Avalon's magic with you."

"I'll bring it back," I said.

"Makes no difference to me. I have a thousand faces. One less won't mean much."

He gestured for us to step aboard. The raft bore our weight, though water did get in my shoes.

He pushed us off, and the boat sailed away on its own. "What's the plan, then?"

"Surprised you care," said Irene.

"Curiosity," he replied.

"Surprised you're curious," said Irene.

He laughed as the cold fog of the lake closed in around us. "Some things are unusual enough to draw even my attention."

I said, "I use the sword to scare Monty away. I get my gun back from Horace. I bring Viv's sword back to Avalon."

"That's more of an outline than a plan," said the Boatman.

"I'm not great with plans," I said. "Coming up with one would be a waste of time anyway. I don't understand any of this. Not really. I'm hoping all the magic stuff will sort itself out in the end."

"And are you concerned at all that you're taking Avalon's magic from its safe haven, decaying as that safe haven might be, and perhaps placing it in the hands of a nihilistic madman? A madman who *does* understand this magic stuff, who has already nearly killed you, who very well could kill you this time?"

"I hadn't thought of that," I admitted.

"And what if he claims the sword?" asked the Boatman. "Is he not a sword-bearer himself?"

I shivered as the water became ice and yet the raft skimmed along without slowing.

"I survived the Siege Perilous," I said.

"Well, goody for you."

Horace's patio came into view, and the boat almost capsized when striking the pool's edge. Irene and I jumped off. The Boatman was already gone by the time I looked back.

Horace's house sat atop a hill. You could see the town below. He would sometimes sit by the pool at night, surveying the twinkling lights, imagining it as his personal kingdom.

There were a lot fewer lights than usual tonight. Fires burned here and there. The biggest buildings in the skyline were dark shadows. The Dragon's shadow swam through the black sky. I felt its hunger and rage, but it was kept at bay by Horace and the power of the gun. But the city below was still ruins.

"This doesn't make any sense," I said. "I gave Horace the gun to keep this from happening."

Irene said, "This isn't the Dragon. This is Horace's shitty soul manifested through a broken power. Everything goes to hell."

"Are we too late?"

"Hard to say. What we're seeing might be the end. Or it might be a glimpse of what's to come."

Horace's house was falling to pieces, as if it had been sitting here for a thousand years without any care, but it refused to collapse. The pool tile cracked beneath our every step. The trees were half-dead. I slid the glass door leading into the house, and it broke off in my hand then fell off the track.

Against my better judgment, we went into the crumbling house. There was no sign of Monty, but a few goons lurked in the darkened corners. They moved back and forth like hungry but cautious wild animals in their ragged clothes.

Every stick of furniture, every piece of glass, was broken. Holes and tears had been punched in the walls. I stepped on a picture frame. It was a photo of Horace and Irene's mom, rent in two. I must have seen the photo dozens of times, and Horace never looked happy in it. But it might have been the happiest he ever had been. Now it was just so much garbage in a fallen house.

None of the people—if that was even what they were—attacked us as we made our way into the study. Horace sat behind his lopsided desk. The Dragon allowed moonlight to pour through a hole in the ceiling, casting a dim spotlight on him, though his face remained in shadow. A layer of dust covered everything.

He took a long drink out of a whiskey bottle. Some spilled across his shirt and jacket, but there were already too many stains to count.

"I was wondering when you'd come back, Ortiz."

He leaned forward. Sallow flesh wrapped his face in a permanent sneer. Half his teeth were missing, and the half remaining were cracked and yellow. I could smell his rotten breath from across the room.

I said, "Jesus, Horace, you look like shit."

"You can't have it back." He wiped his runny nose with the back of his hand. He glanced at the gun, placed his hand near it. "It's mine."

"You have to know what's happening," I said. "You're going full Gollum."

He grunted. "I don't watch that fairy tale fantasy bullshit."

Irene said, "Look at this place. Look at you. The longer you hold onto that gun, the worse it is for everyone. I know you're a real asshole, Horace, but this can't be what you want. To sit on a throne in a world in ruins?"

"It's what the world has always been when you strip away all the lies. Just a shithole where everyone is looking out for themselves."

That summarized the problem. Horace had a lot of hate in his soul. Enough hate to turn the world into a wasteland. It was possible the corrupted magic in the sword was also responsible. I didn't understand it enough to say. But whatever was happening, there was only one way to stop it.

"I'm going to take that away from you," I said. "And we both know there's nothing you can do about it."

He smiled with all the rotten glee in his rotten heart. "And then what? I'm keeping that thing in the sky away. Without me, the world dies."

"Maybe letting it die is better than this," I said.

Horace grabbed the gun off his desk. Tried to. It wouldn't budge. He couldn't use it against me. I let him try for a few more moments before, out of breath, he fell back into his chair. He took another drink then threw the bottle against the wall.

"You're not better than me."

"He's not the guy decomposing in his own filth like a twisted version of the Fisher King," said Irene.

Horace sighed. "You always did act like that arts degree made you smarter than me."

"Oh, I was smarter than you long before that. And Ortiz is a better guy. Not that that's hard. Everybody is."

The air rippled before us as Monty appeared. His body of light was almost blinding in the gray. Even more striking, he wore an immaculate suit. "It's touching family moments like this that make it all worthwhile."

"About time you showed up," said Horace. "Kill these stupid assholes already."

Monty, hands in pockets, sat on the desk. "I don't work for you."

"You need me," said Horace.

"Do I?" Monty studied me. "So you survived the Siege Perilous, Ortiz. I'm impressed. How did you not die?"

"I cheated," I said.

"Whatever works."

The world trembled with the Dragon roar. The house didn't collapse. To collapse would be a mercy, and there wasn't any mercy left under Horace's reign. Death and destruction often sucked, but with them gone, there was only an eternal in-between. A world without endings had no beginnings.

Viv's sword materialized in my hand. Its inner light caused both Monty and Horace to recoil. "You can't stop me this time."

Horace snorted. "Look at king shit all of a sudden. You never had any balls, Ortiz. Holding that sword doesn't change that."

"I'll use it if I have to."

"That's the thing guys like you never understand. It's not *if*. It's never *if*. You have power. You use it. Otherwise, what's the point of having the power?"

"Spoken like a true scumbag," said Irene.

"He's not the one who will destroy the world," said Monty. "You sense it, don't you, Ortiz? The Dragon is enraged. The cycle is broken. The moment you take the gun from Horace it will descend on this world with all its fury. Nothing will be left behind. Not even ashes. This is the choice."

He was manipulating me, but that didn't make him wrong. Before I found my sword, I was just a loser, not worth a damn. After I'd found it, I was still a loser. All I'd done since was make things worse. Monty hadn't made Horace a linchpin of the universe. That was me.

Irene put her hand on my shoulder. "We're all idiots. Monty and Horace. Viv. Hell, I've become the embodiment of wisdom, and I feel like I know less than ever. It's not about being smart or strong or certain. It's about being the right person to make the right decision at the right time."

"How do I know I'm the right person?" I asked.

The light of cosmic fire in my eyes reflected off her own. I lost myself in the swirling colors.

"You have the sword, don't you?"

"Hell of a pep talk." Monty flared brighter. "But the way I see it, you can run away back to Avalon, eke out whatever happiness you can. Or you can kill me. But we're bound, so you'll die, too. There will be no bearer for the gun. One choice ends with the end of everything. One with the world like this."

He walked up to me, letting the tip of the sword press against his chest. He leaned into it enough to tear his suit jacket. Little globules of light bubbled up from a shallow wound.

"It's up to you to decide what you can live with."

He didn't fear me. It wasn't that he didn't think I'd do it. He just didn't care. The Gorge had taken every bit of humanity from him. All that was left was a shell, no different than the decaying house around us. He didn't want to live, but neither did he care about dying. It was all the same to him.

I drove the sword through him. It didn't take much. Just a push, and it sliced through his body like the light it was made of. We screamed as one, both collapsed to our knees. Monty's body of light sputtered and flickered like a dying flame. He spit up globules of phosphorescent vomit.

The wound on his chest hemorrhaged light in fluttering strands.

"I'm sorry," I wheezed with a collapsed lung.

He smiled painfully. "I know you are."

His life floated away in a rainbow of colors. His body dissolved, leaving an empty suit, as we died.

CHAPTER TWENTY-THREE

I sat up. Blood soaked my shirt, mirroring the wound I'd inflicted on Monty. I hurt like hell, and I could hear the air whistling through my lungs when I breathed too deeply. But I wasn't dead.

Irene offered me a hand up.

"Did you know?" I asked.

"Had a hunch," she replied. "But I'm carrying wisdom, not knowledge, so I didn't know for sure."

I hadn't died in Avalon because it was an eternal place where death didn't belong, but I hadn't died here because death was kept at bay by Horace and that gun. In Avalon, my wounds had healed. In Horace's kingdom, they remained.

The pain ran through me as I continued to bleed, but the way Horace had broken the world, pain was a given. I was aware of myself as a decaying piece of meat, stuck in the freezer. Fuzz was on the package, and you'd be crazy to eat it, but it was easy to ignore sitting in the back. That was death here, too lazy to take out the trash.

"If you couldn't die, how did Monty?" asked Irene.

"I don't think he did," I said. "I can feel him, like he's here but not. The sword disrupted him. Should be long enough for us to do what we need to do."

Horace coughed up a dry wheeze, reminding us of his presence. He went for the gun. Again. He couldn't lift it. He must have known that. The need to have it overwrote his reason. It was pure animalistic want. The same hunger that had driven him his whole life.

He used both hands, his back straining, his knees shaking. "You're nobody, Ortiz. You never should have had this in the first place."

His trembling body and ragged voice countered any attempts to be intimidating. Hard to believe I'd spent years being afraid of this guy. He grunted and growled like a beast. The Dragon's wings covered the moon, casting a scarlet glow on everything. "If you take this gun from me, you'll die."

I replied, "I've gotten pretty good at cheating death. And if I have to die to fix the mess I made, it might be the only worthwhile thing I've ever done."

"You didn't make the mess," said Irene. "You inherited it. It was a mess long before you showed up."

Horace rattled out a chuckle. "You have no fucking clue. The Dragon will eat everything, burn it all to ash."

He coughed, spitting up phlegm and blood. The gun burned his flesh now, and still, he couldn't let it go.

I said to Irene, "You don't have to watch this."

"No. I should be here. I'm his only family."

"Let her watch." He tilted his head down to wipe his mouth on his shoulder. "Ungrateful little brat probably getting off on it."

She looked at him with pity. His face fell as he saw himself as she saw him. He'd been clawing for respect and power his whole life, and to be seen as this pathetic thing broke him, deep down. He yowled, scratching at the gun as sweat ran down his reddened face.

She said, "I know there's no love lost between us, but . . ."

She couldn't find the words to finish that sentence. They'd been at each other's throats for years, but he'd been there for her as a kid. He'd been a lousy father, but still, not the worst. And he'd probably cared for her as much as he could.

"Just finish it, Ortiz." She didn't turn away.

I picked up the gun. It resisted, but it didn't have a choice. Because I was its bearer.

Horace fell back in his chair. His breath grew shallow and his body damp and limp. He was all used up. Only powerless rage remained. Dying embers flickering behind his eyes. Hate—even impotent hate—could keep a man going long after their body has gone.

He rasped, "At least I was something before you gave me that sword. Who the fuck are you? Still a nobody, even with it. I'd rather be hated than forgotten. It'll be a long time before—"

"Hey, why don't you do me a favor and shut up?" I said.

He glared. Then half-smiled. "Now who's the asshole?"

The Dragon roared as it tore off the roof with one swipe of its claws. It reached down and snatched Horace out of his chair. There was no fight left in him. I'd taken back more than the gun. I'd taken his soul, consumed by the boon but withered away long before that. The Dragon considered him with an alien curiosity. It tossed him away like a piece of garbage. Horace bounced off the desk, crumpling in a twisted heap on the floor.

He wheezed, his chest rising and falling. Still, he didn't die. It was like the Dragon was denying him that mercy.

I aimed the gun between his eyes, and he offered a derisive wet laugh at the joke. He'd always known it would end this way, but that it was me pulling the trigger . . . well . . . it was funny. Just not funny ha-ha.

I pulled the trigger. The power of the gun blew away half his skull. I worried it might not be enough to finish the job, and he did twitch a couple of times. But then, mercifully, he died.

The house rattled as it came down around our heads. Irene took me by the hand and led me through the collapse. Chunks of ceiling fell around us, but she always knew where to walk. A crumbling wall buried two thugs. A faux-classic pillar toppled on another. Irene led me with slow, steady guidance around the mayhem, and a few steps after exiting into the back patio, the entire house fell in on itself.

The world quaked as the Dragon rose from the rubble. It fixed us with its burning eyes, spreading wide its glittering wings. The Dragon raised up, massive as a mountain, and bellowed its rage. It slammed back to earth, raking the ground with its claws of fire. I pulled Irene close as it leaned down. Its hot breath washed over us. The pool bubbled and boiled.

"No hard feelings?" I asked more than said.

The Dragon closed its jaws. It snorted, turning away. It toppled several trees with a casual swish of its tail before vanishing.

"Is it gone?" said Irene.

"It's never gone, but it's back where it belongs. That shadow of death lurking just over our shoulder."

Pain stabbed me in my chest. Irene caught me before I fell over. She strained to keep me on my feet.

"What's wrong?" she asked.

I tried saying something, but I couldn't breathe. A sword wound through your chest could do that. Death was back in the game. The magic of Avalon kept me alive, but it was waning. I didn't know what would happen to Viv's sword or mine when I died, but it would sort itself out. It wouldn't be my problem anyway.

"We have to get you back to Avalon." Irene did her best to drag me toward the pool, but I tripped on shattered tile, and fell to the ground. I couldn't get my legs to work, but Irene, bless her, grabbed me by the collar and pulled me inch by inch.

"Come on, you stupid asshole." She grunted and strained. "You're crazy if you think I'm going to let you die now."

"Love you, too," I said.

Actually, I gargled with two lungs full of my own blood, but she got the message.

The Boatman appeared in the mists at the pool's edge, Gwen standing in the bow.

"Help me," Irene said. "Please."

"I don't get off the boat," he replied. "It's in the name."

Gwen stepped off the boat. She dipped her cup in the pool and knelt beside me.

"Will it work?" asked Irene.

"One way to find out." Gwen pressed the cup into my hand. The magic of the Siege Perilous tingled in my fingertips. She helped me lift the cup to my mouth. The hot water seared my tongue as I drank, but the burns healed a moment later.

"That tastes awful," I said. That I could say anything was a good sign.

"Pool water," said Gwen. "Now just shut up and drink."

She poured the entire cup of chlorinated elixir down my throat. By the end I was restored and energized. I practically jumped to my feet.

Irene hugged me, then slapped me, then hugged me. "You gotta stop dying, you idiot."

"I'll work on it."

The city below remained dark. One of the distant fires flickered and extinguished. A small, hopeful thing.

The Boatman cleared his throat. "Not to put a rush on anything, but we should probably get Viv's sword back to her before Avalon perishes."

We boarded the raft and pushed off into the mists.

CHAPTER TWENTY-FOUR

The trip itself was a short passage through a dark tunnel. Avalon didn't have enough magic for anything more interesting.

As Avalon came into view, it was obvious that we hadn't fixed whatever we'd broken. The skies above were gray and the forest withered. A shroud covered the Boatman. One of his hands was skeletal, and his dry, cracked voice worked like a hot poker in my eardrums.

"Last stop."

I didn't know how literally he meant it, and I didn't ask.

We made our way to the castle, which had diminished from impossible grandeur to merely a big old fortress. Bricks fell from the crumbling towers as we approached. Vultures circled overhead. The sweet odor of lightly rotting meat drifted in the air.

We found Viv slumped in the throne room. She must have dragged herself there. Once grand, now it was small, dark, and cold. Water dribbled from a leak in the ceiling, forming a brackish puddle beside the throne. She lay there looking not much different than Horace had in his final moments. Except Horace's final moments were full of hate. She carried hers with quiet acceptance.

I materialized her sword and placed it in her hand. Her fingers wrapped loosely around it.

I shook her lightly, afraid she might break. "I'm giving it back. It's yours again."

She opened her eyes and smiled. Her lips parted as if to say something.

"It's not working," I said.

"She might be too weak to take it back," said Gwen.

"Use the cup," said Irene.

Gwen collected some stagnant water in her cup. She put it to Viv's lips, who drank it. Nothing happened.

"Why isn't it working?" I asked.

"Boons don't work for bearers," said Gwen.

"It worked for me."

"You're the exception," she said. "You survived the Siege Perilous."

"So we'll put her in it," I said.

"It would kill her," said Irene.

"No one dies in Avalon," I said.

A quake shook the island, and a chunk of the ceiling collapsed.

"I don't think that's true anymore," said Irene.

"Come on." I laid her sword across her lap and squeezed her fingers around the handle. "Come on."

Irene put her hand on my shoulder. "It's not your fault. Avalon was dying long before you came along."

"Maybe it's destiny," added Gwen. "Nothing lasts forever. Maybe nothing should."

"Fuck that," I said.

Irene put her arm around me. "Ortiz . . ."

"No. I'm not accepting that."

"You don't have a choice," said Irene.

"No." I pulled away from her. "My whole life I've accepted that the world was shit, and that's probably the way it will always be. But not here. Maybe everything else sucks, but not here."

I shoved the sword against Viv and wrapped her arms around it. "Take the goddamn sword already!"

Her eyes snapped open, no longer small and dark, but large and red. Like my eyes. Like Monty's eyes.

"Oh, shit," said Irene.

Viv stood, but it wasn't her.

"Viv?" I asked.

Her eyes flashed an all too familiar red as her body burned away. Monty stood in her place.

"You son of a bitch." I took a step toward him and wound up with his sword at my throat.

"Care to try your luck cheating death again?" He grinned. "I told you. I can't die. I wonder . . . if I stabbed you with this, would you? Or would you find yourself drawn into the blade like I was?"

"You used the sword to sneak a ride," said Irene.

"All this time, we've been bearing these boons, and no one ever thought to ask if they could carry us. Although even that would only work if I had another sword-bearer to bring me along. One invited into Avalon. Which you were kind enough to do, Ortiz."

"This was your plan all along," I said.

He laughed. "Plan? What makes you think any of this was planned? This is us, little sacks of flesh, struggling to make sense of an impossible world. But now I see the sense. I finally get it. I'm here to brave the Siege Perilous."

He flicked the sword, drawing blood with a shallow cut on my neck. He snapped his fingers and jagged pillars like the Dragon's teeth pushed through the floor and ceiling, separating us from him.

"You won't survive it," called Gwen through a gap.

"Well, that's my problem, isn't it?" He saluted and walked away.

We searched the halls of Avalon, not getting anywhere.

"Don't you know the way?" I asked Irene.

"It's not my way to find," she replied.

"So what's the problem?" said Gwen. "If he finds the Siege, it will just kill him. Or trap him forever. None of us are going to get him out of it."

"Can we take that chance?" I said. "He might be worthy."

"He's a nutjob," said Irene. "Why would he be worthy?"

"He's pure," I said.

"What the hell does that mean?"

"His goals are simple, directed. He's not confused. The sword and the Gorge might have screwed with his head, but they also made him more focused. He wants power. He wants it for its own sake, and I think the Siege will give it to him."

"Then what can we do about it?" said Irene. "Avalon is under his command. If he doesn't want us to stop him, we won't stop him."

"That's not quite right," said Gwen. "Avalon obeys, but it isn't a slave. It took Viv centuries to gain command over it, and even then, it would defy her now and then."

"I need your staff," I told Irene.

She materialized it. "Now what?"

I closed my eyes as I touched the staff. It wasn't Irene's way to find, but I was connected to Monty, the sword, the Dragon, the Siege Perilous. They'd all taken a piece of me and left something else in return.

I pointed to a door that wasn't there five seconds ago. "There."

We opened the door and came across Monty standing beside the Siege. We couldn't reach him in time.

"It won't give you what you want," said Irene.

"She bears the staff," said Gwen. "Maybe you should listen to her."

"Maybe I should." He braced himself on the Siege Perilous, holding himself mid-sit. "But it seems a shame to have come this far and not take the chance."

Monty sat. He screamed as his body flared like a miniature sun. Avalon quaked as the Siege burned through the floor, falling into the dark depths below.

The screaming faded. I didn't hear him hit the bottom. Maybe there was no bottom to hit. He'd burn forever, fall forever.

The floor felt as unstable as the castle and the ground it was built upon.

I said, "He didn't deserve that."

"He made his choice," said Gwen.

"What choice did he ever make?" I said. "First, the sword took control of him. Then you pushed him into a hole that ate his humanity. He was just a guy, like the rest of us."

She shrugged. "We can point fingers all we want, but it's over."

"It's not over." The sword materialized in my hand. It poked and prodded at my brain. It wanted to be used. It was ready to be used. "It's never over."

The floor fell away revealing the bottomless chasm underneath. We stepped away from the precarious edge, but there was nowhere safe to go. Not really.

"Isn't there a sleeping dragon under there?" said Irene.

A pillar of fire blasted from the darkness, exploding through the ceiling. The foundations shook as the primeval beast clawed its way toward the surface.

"Jörmungandr," said Gwen. "The end of the world."

Irene said, "Well, that sucks."

A hungry laugh bubbled up from the pit as the Dragon climbed closer. It sounded impossibly far away, but also, just right here. The embodiment of the thing you put off until tomorrow, and then tomorrow is suddenly here.

"You have to go," I said.

"Where can we go? Didn't you hear her? It's the end of the fucking world." Irene sounded perturbed as she lit a cigarette. "Might as well have a front-row seat."

I tightened my grip on my sword. It filled me with an ungodly amount of strength. A great claw reached over the edge. Its scales glittered like a rainbow. Irene and Gwen averted their eyes, but I couldn't help but be drawn to it. This was what the sword was for. This was what I was for.

"Just go," I said. "Please."

"Ortiz, I'm not leaving you."

The sword wanted me to strike her down for her defiance, but the sword could go screw itself.

The Dragon's giant head rose from the pit. It was a beautiful chaos with a crown of silver and black horns. Fire erupted from its nostrils with each breath, and acidic saliva dripped from its terrible maw.

But its eyes blazed with all the power of its hungry soul.

It spoke with a voice it shouldn't have. With Monty's voice.

"Hello, Ortiz."

I pointed the sword at his throat. "We don't have to do this."

"Oh, but isn't it what we're made to do?"

The Dragon pulled himself halfway out of the pit. He exhaled an inferno. I split the flames with the sword, and jumped forward. Right into his mouth. He snapped me up, swallowing me whole.

I floated in the infinite void. The Dragon lived in the Gorge, but the Gorge lived in the Dragon. But I had the sword now, and it couldn't hold me. I stabbed the dark, slicing an escape, dragging myself through the wound back into the world. I fell into the castle as the Dragon, its split neck spewing sparkling gore, tumbled back into the chasm.

Glittering viscera covered me, like an unholy combination of warrior and stripper.

"Holy shit," said Irene. "When did you become a badass?"

"It's not me," I said. "It's the sword."

The chasm rumbled as the Dragon clawed his way back to the surface. He was bigger now. Meaner. Hungrier. He spread his crimson wings. Half the walls collapsed, and it was only through its enchanted nature that the castle stayed standing.

"What did the Siege do to you?" I asked.

"It showed me the truth. The boons are not tools for humanity. Humanity is the tool, a way for the boons to become gods."

"You're not a god," I said.

"No, I am much more than that. But you already know that. You and that sword."

He pulled himself all the way out of the hole. Every step threatened to split the earth. Up to now, the Dragon had been rage and power, but simple in its desires. It wanted to fight whoever carried the sword. But it wasn't malice. It was just a reaction. Like chemistry or physics. Two ancient forces revolving around one another.

Now that Monty was in charge it was giving a natural disaster a mind of its own. It was giving that asteroid that killed the dinosaurs greater ambitions.

"The Dragon is fucking with your head," I said. "You don't have to give in to it."

"Give in?" He advanced on us with the reassured gait of an apex predator. "Is that what you actually think? Power is to be used. Why would I have it if not to use it? Just as you have that sword to use."

"We're bearers," said Gwen. "We bear the burdens. We don't use them."

"Ah, yes. Power corrupts. Perhaps it does, but I welcome it. Because this shit feels amazing."

Faster than the eye could follow, he tried to crush me beneath his foot, but it was all slow motion to me. I sliced off the limb, then threw the sword into his chest. Howling, he disintegrated into a pile of rainbow sludge.

A moment later, the Dragon rose up from the pit again.

"You can't beat me," he said. "Destroy me a thousand times, and I'll be reborn stronger every time."

The sword filled me with more strength. Enough to match Monty and just a little bit more. Always just a little bit more.

"I can keep killing you," I said.

"Yes, we could do this until the end of time and beyond. The two of us, alone in the emptiness. Two immortals, bound together forever in the ruins. It does sound like fun."

He lunged, and I drove the sword between his eyes. The corpse hadn't finished dissolving this time before a fresh version emerged from the chasm. His mere act of breathing caused the sky above Avalon to crack and the ground to shake.

And still more strength came to me.

Unlimited.

Just enough.

Too much.

The sword was its own hurricane, swirling around in my brain, stirring up instincts I didn't know I had because I'd never had the option before. I was never the important guy in the room. Now I was the most important guy.

"We were chosen for this." Monty lowered his head before me, and the sword screamed to deliver another killing blow. But it seemed pointless, and I pushed the alien thoughts away.

"I can't let you destroy the world."

"Why would I want to do that? What's the point in being a god without toys? But we needn't squabble among ourselves. Allow me to break the universe into pieces and glue those pieces together in new and amusing ways. And in return, I'll leave Avalon."

"Avalon is dying," said Gwen.

"If I leave, it will return to its former glory. You can rebuild it."

"A truce?" asked Irene. "And the rest of the world can go to hell?"

The Dragon narrowed its eyes with unmistakable disgust, as if listening to her was like a bug crawling through its ears. "Beats the alternative. You were nothing, Ortiz. An idiot. A fool. Yours was a sad little life destined for a sad little death until you found that sword and freed me from the Gorge. This is your chance to be happy, and why should you care what happens to anyone or anything else? They never cared what happened to you."

The sword grumbled in my head. It wanted the fight, needed it. I lowered the blade.

"You can't be seriously considering this," said Irene.

"These are his choices," said Monty. "Makes no difference to me which one he chooses."

I turned to Irene, and only now realized I was twice as big as her. If I kept fighting, I'd keep getting bigger and bigger until I was big enough to step on her. And I wouldn't even notice.

"You're not a bad guy, Ortiz," she said.

"No, but I'm not a good guy either." I knelt down, but didn't touch her. If I wasn't careful, I'd crush her purely by accident. "I'm just an idiot who found a sword."

I threw myself into Monty. Together, we tumbled down into the void below.

I couldn't say how long we fell, but we landed hard. The Dragon exploded on impact, unleashing a shower of sparkles. My body shattered. It should have killed me, but a lot of things should have killed me lately. It was just one more on the list. I lay in a broken heap in the cavernous dark until my body decided to fix itself. One moment, there was pain. The next, I stood up without an ache.

Monty, his body blazing like a pyre, appeared before me.

The sword in my hand glowed with its own inner light.

"You're a fool, Ortiz." He spread his wings but couldn't fly away. The only way out, metaphysically, was past me. "But if you want this, then so be it."

He moved to attack, but I held up my hand. The gesture caused him to pause mid-strike.

"I never wanted to be important," I said. "I just wanted something more, but not this. I know you can't understand that. I must seem so insignificant. And I'll admit that it's tempting. All this power at my fingertips. I'll admit that even now the sword is poking and prodding and tell me to fight.

"But I don't want to fight. It's pointless. I know we got off to a bad start, but we don't have to keep doing this. We don't have to like each other. Lots of people don't like me."

The Dragon snorted curiously.

I said, "But we can live together. We can put aside the pissing contest, and just coexist. Believe me, it's possible. I've been doing it my whole life. I'll go first."

I placed the sword at my feet. It screamed, not metaphorically, but really screamed as I willed my hand to let it go. The sword refused to fall from my grasp, clinging to my palm with supernatural resistance. I shook my hand like a man trying to flick away some unwanted sticky bit of goop. The Dragon watched with mild curiosity.

"Just give me a second." I pinned the blade flat on the ground with my foot and pulled. The flesh peeled away from the sword's handle. I stepped away as the buzz saw chatter in my head quieted to bearable levels.

"There. Done."

Monty yawned. "Is this your proposal? A fragile peace between rivals?"

"I wasn't talking to you," I said.

He snarled as he prepared to stomp me flat, but the claw never fell. It only hung there over my head.

Monty roared and tried again. The results were the same. Over and over, each attack ended before it began. His fire died in his throat. His limbs refused to obey. I stood there, hands in pockets, watching him struggle.

"How?" he asked.

"The Dragon fights the sword," I replied. "You and me, we're just tools."

Through the connection, I felt the rage in the Dragon ebb, and as it ebbed, the power of the sword faded. I felt Monty's mind pushing against the Dragon, trying to stoke its aggression. But he was just a small mind riding a dying tornado.

"You haven't won," he said, but his voice was fading as the endless sleep started to take the Dragon again.

"We never win," I said. "We just survive."

"Oh, fuck you."

The Dragon lowered its head, folded its wings, and drifted into a fitful sleep. Monty fell asleep, and I hoped that he found some peace.

I left the sword behind and started walking. It wasn't long before I came across a chasm wall. The sheer cliff stretched for miles, but it was possible to climb it. I didn't have the strength of the sword any more, but I might be able to make it.

I grabbed a rocky outcropping and pulled myself up.

"Hey, dumbass." Irene stood at the foot of a staircase that I could've sworn wasn't there before. "Did you save the world or not?"

"I didn't destroy it."

She shrugged, helped me off the wall. "Well, I guess that's close enough."

CHAPTER TWENTY-FIVE

The stairs started out as uneven rough stone carved from the rock. A few dozen steps up and they smoothed. Another dozen, they transformed into sloppy brickwork. The bricks straightened as an elaborate railing grew from the earth. By the time we reached the top, intricate images were carved along the path. They depicted a great battle between a dragon and a mighty hero, ending only when the hero laid down his sword.

Irene elbowed me. "Look at that. You're a legend now."

"Legends are overrated," said Gwen from the top of the stairs.

We stepped out of the depths and into the castle's treasury, filled with mountains of riches. Chests overflowed with jewels. Golden statues. The whole shebang.

"How long were we down there?" I asked.

"What's time in the Dreaming World?" said Gwen. "You put the Dragon back to sleep. Avalon is reborn."

She led us into another chamber. This one was just as big, and at its center, a giant round table made of granite. A massive tapestry hung behind the biggest chair. The weaving was so fine it was like looking at a photograph. Its subject was me, sitting on a throne, while a sword was suspended above my head.

"Sword of Damocles," I said.

"Where the hell did you pick that up?" asked Irene.

"I'll tell you later. So I'm king now?"

"Do you want to be king?" said Gwen.

"Hell no."

I said it without hesitation, but the truth was that there was a part of me that did want that. Hadn't I earned it? But that wasn't the question that needed to be asked.

"I'm not worthy," I said.

"Nobody's worthy," said Irene. "But you did it, Ortiz."

"I didn't do anything," I said. "I just put down the sword."

Gwen said, "That sword's promises took hold of Monty and every soul to ever touch it. But not you." She studied me like a curious puzzle. "Somehow."

"I'm as surprised as you," I said.

"I'm not." Irene rematerialized her staff for effect. She did look wiser with it. "Don't you get it, Jay? Your complete lack of ambition was kryptonite to the sword."

"I wouldn't say complete," I replied.

"Let's just say what ambition is in there is woefully underdeveloped." She smiled, and I took it as the compliment it was intended to be.

A smokeless white flame burned along the edges of the tapestry dedicated to my glory. Seemed a shame to see it go, but I didn't need it.

"A man without dreams." Gwen shrugged. "Whatever works."

"If I'm not going to be king, what happens to Avalon now that Viv is gone?" I asked.

"Who says Viv is gone?"

The next room was smaller. A sparkling pool sat at its center, and a school of white and gold fish in a humanoid shape swam just below the surface.

Gwen said, "Avalon endures, as does its Lady. It will put her back together eventually."

"The castle is rebuilt almost instantly, but Viv will take a while," said Irene.

"The Dreaming World has its own rules."

The fish broke formation and swam to the pool's edge. I dipped my fingers in, and they nibbled. A particularly big fish with Viv's dark eyes gazed up at me, playfully spitting a small stream into my face.

"Yeah, you're welcome." I splashed the pool, and the fish scattered.

"So you don't want to be king," said Gwen. "What do you want?"

"I could go for a beer," I said. "Maybe some pizza rolls."

Smiling, Gwen led us into the next room. It was smaller than all the others, and nothing special to look at other than the long table, set with many beers and a variety of pizza rolls.

She waved her arm at the feast. "Avalon provides."

I grabbed a bottle of some imported brand of beer I'd never heard of. The castle was trying its best, and it didn't really matter at the moment. The bottle opened itself, and I took a long drink.

We stayed in Avalon for a while. How long was anybody's guess. We only went outside to watch the sunsets, and it was always sunset when we went out. Gwen left at some point, and it was just me and Irene alone in a big magical castle that gave us everything we could want. We lived on beer and pizza rolls and whatever else Avalon provided in its gratitude.

We slept in. We made love. Unashamedly, without self-consciousness, because Avalon was the kind of place people made love.

I would have stayed there forever. I'd saved Avalon and put the Dragon back to sleep, but I couldn't shake the feeling that the damage outside of this place was more permanent. Maybe the Waking World had been consumed in atomic fire. Maybe it was just shittier than it had been. Either way, I didn't want to know.

But Irene—never one to let common sense get in her way—was curious. I talked her out of it for as long as I could, but eventually, we walked to the shore and waited for the Boatman.

"You don't have to come," she said.

"You're my guide," I replied. "I go where you go. But if it sucks, I'm coming back, with or without you."

"I'd expect no less."

The Boatman appeared through the mists. He was tall and broad with a drawn but handsome face. With Avalon's magic restored, his boat was large and sturdy. He lowered the gangplank. "All aboard."

"What's it like out there?" I asked as we climbed onto the boat.

Without saying a word, he pushed off.

The Boatman dropped us off at a local pool. We got a few curious looks, but they faded as he disappeared back into the ether.

At a glance, the Waking World was okay.

A longer visit showed that maybe it was a little better than okay.

People walked down the street with smiles. The sky was bluer. The sun was bright; but also, gentle.

Everything felt just a little better.

"This is because of you," said Irene. "The threat of the Dragon and the power of that sword hung over this world. These people didn't know it, but they felt it, deep down. It's like this metaphysical weight has been lifted off humanity's shoulders."

"I've made everyone nicer? So I did actually save the world?"

She pulled me close. "Not bad for a guy without ambition."

Two cars collided in the street. It wasn't more than a fender bender, but both drivers started screaming at one another.

"Okay, so maybe you didn't save it." She kissed me. "But maybe with some time, the human race can finally become something better than it is. Who knows how this stuff works? Not me. And I'm wise."

We walked through the Waking World. Or the Dreaming World. Or both. An arbitrary distinction, but whatever world we were in wasn't burning any more, and that was enough.

Back at my apartment, outside the window, the city looked different. It gleamed with hope and possibility. It might have been only a symbolic reflection. Or maybe a glimpse into the future. But it held promise.

I opened the door to my bathroom, only to find the room was empty of every fixture except for the Siege Perilous and the sword propped next to it.

"You about ready?" asked Irene from the kitchen.

"One second."

I entered the bathroom and closed the door behind me. The chair and the sword whispered to me. I might not have had any grand ambitions, but I was human. Wanting more was normal. Wanting it all was foolish.

But with the sword . . .

I looked down at my hand reaching for it and took back control.

This was the Sword of Damocles, hanging over my head, whispering to me of the greatness that could be mine. This was the Siege Perilous, offering me dreams undreamed if only I was willing to have a seat and endure its challenge.

Irene knocked on the door. "You okay in there?"

"Yeah, I'm okay." I put my hands in my pockets and shook my head at the sword. "You can fuck right off," I whispered back.

The sword offered a psychic chuckle. It had all the time in the world for me to give in. I didn't know if I could resist it forever, but I could resist it for today. And tomorrow.

The week after that . . .

I'd worry about that then.

I squeezed out of the bathroom, opening and closing the door quickly enough that Irene didn't get a good look.

"I still don't know why we came back here," she said. "We can go anywhere in the world, we're blessed by the universe, and you want to take one last look at this dump?"

"It's not so bad. I think I'll keep it."

"Why the hell would you want to do that?"

"If I'm supposed to bear this responsibility, it's better to be part of the world than in some faraway mythical castle."

"Faraway castles don't have bedbugs, at least."

"Bedbugs keep me humble."

"I feel there's a middle ground somewhere."

"Probably. We'll figure it out."

I took her in my arms and kissed her. She wasn't always easy to get along with, but I was glad she was here. The sword promised me power, but with Irene, there was always someone to remind me that kind of power was the last thing I needed.

"Hey." She stammered, sucked in a long, deep breath, then spit out the next part in one garbled syllable. "I love you."

"Are you sure about that?"

"Screw you." Grinning, she punched me in the shoulder. Hard. "A guy sort of maybe saves the world and suddenly he's an asshole."

"Sort of maybe saving the world does do that to a guy."

I took her hand in mine. "Ready to go?"

"Where to?"

"Wherever we want."

I opened the door.